OUT THERE, IN THE FOREST

Two Plays

Shmuel Cohavy

OUT THERE
IN THE FOREST

Two Plays

Shmuel Cohavy

SAMUEL WACHTMAN'S SONS

DEKEL PUBLISHING HOUSE

OUT THERE, IN THE FOREST
Two Plays

SHMUEL COHAVY

Copyright © 2014

Dekel Academic Press
www.dekelpublishing.com

North American rights by
Samuel Wachtman's Sons, Inc.
ISBN 978-1-888820-84-3

Editor:	Zvi Morik
Language editing:	Kathleen Roman

Cover image: Pulpitis © Wooden Bridge Through The Mangrove Reforestation Photo, Dreamstime.com

Cover design and typesetting by

For information contact:

Dekel Publishing House
P.O. Box 45094
Tel Aviv 6145002, Israel
Tel: +972 3506-3235
Fax: +972 3506-7332
Email: info@dekelpublishing.com

Samuel Wachtman's Sons, Inc.
2460 Garden Road, Suite C
Monterey, CA 93940, U.S.A.
Tel: 831 649-0669
Fax: 831 649-8007
Email: samuelwachtman@gmail.com

CONTENTS

EIN RO'EEM

A play by Shmuel Cohavy

Scene 1

Kibbutz Ein Ro'eem—the central lawn and the head office. Enters Zoltty, the head of the kibbutz's Financial Board, and Doobi.

Zoltty

> I've done a lot for you, Doobi. Don't forget that you weren't born in the kibbutz. You came here as a child and you got a foster family. Like your foster family, I myself adopted you in many ways. I sent you to courses, I made you a member of the kibbutz's Financial Board, and I made you a head of the junior section in Ein Ro'eem. Don't forget it.

Doobi

> You remind me that I wasn't born here…

Zoltty

> I don't want to offend you, Doobi. I didn't want you to feel like people here are doing you a favor. I just want to show you how much you've advanced here—and I had a part in it.

Doobi

> And now you want me to pay you back?

Zoltty

> I want you to give something back to the kibbutz, not to me! Doobi, the kibbutz made a decision, and we are all committed to the decisions! It wasn't me who decided. It was decided at the kibbutz meeting!

Doobi

But people say that you rule the meetings, that you don't let anybody speak.

Zoltty

I rule the meetings? Who says that? The people who don't even attend the meetings—most of them are young? They just sit there and—

Doobi

It's not only them…

Zoltty

The ones who don't even come, or do come but don't say a word, don't participate. But later, when the meeting is over, on their way home, only *then* they start speaking. They gather in little groups and start to complain. This is not good and this is not good—but at the meeting…

Doobi

Zoltty, what do you want from me?

Zoltty

Do you have any idea how much money we lose because of the orchard? Not the entire orchard, but… Doobi, you're a member of the Financial Committee—do you read the financial reports?

Doobi

I heard there's a good chance that next year the orchard will be profitable.

Zoltty

That's what they said *last* year!

Doobi

So can't we give it another year or two? People have invested a lot in the orchard!

Zoltty

> It's not just a matter of another year or two. All over the country orchards are being cleared. They're just not profitable!

Doobi

> But things change! I mean—when there's frost in Spain, for instance, it influences the—

Zoltty

> We can't count on *the rain in Spain*, Doobi! Next year…

Doobi

> The workers of the orchard say that no one listens to them.

Zoltty

> But this is exactly the problem! They don't come to the kibbutz meetings! And the decision was made at meeting *and* by the Financial Board!

Doobi

> So, I ask you again—what do you want from me?

Zoltty

> Doobi, you are the head of the junior section in the kibbutz. You can't just step aside during such a tough time in the kibbutz. I want you to talk and listen to Arnon.

Doobi

> So that's why you took me all the way to the head office?

Zoltty

> Yes. I want you to talk to the secretary. As head of the junior section, you should also hear what he has to say. Not only me. Come.
>
> *(Zoltty and Doobi go into the office. Hedva and Sgula enter.)*

Sgula

> I just wanna help…

Hedva

> I don't need any help.

Sgula

> You're constantly daydreaming. What's wrong with you?

Hedva

> Nothing's wrong with me.

Sgula

> What are you dreaming about? You walk around like a… like a…

Hedva

> Nothing's wrong.

Sgula

> What's bothering you?

Hedva

> Why are you so concerned about me?

Sgula

> I want you to come to the rehearsal, and maybe that will snap you out of this mood. I also would like you to be at my side and help me. What do you say?

Hedva

> Help you? How?

Sgula

> You played the role last year. You were the princess. You can watch, comment…

Hedva

> Last year, according to what you say, the show was different. It was—

Sgula

> The story is different, but a princess is a princess, and you were a princess. You can help, correct—

Hedva

>That's the director's job, isn't it?

Sgula

>Ro'ee? He's not very helpful.

Hedva

>Why? Isn't he supportive?

Sgula

>Not really.

Hedva

>What's the problem?

Sgula

>He…I don't know…he's little…

Hedva

>What?

Sgula

>Can I trust you? Not to tell anybody?

Hedva

>Sure!

Sgula

>He made a pass at me.

Hedva

>Seriously!

Sgula

>Yeah.

Hedva

>So? What's wrong with that?

Sgula

>I don't like him.

Hedva

You don't…?

Sgula

No. Not at all.

Hedva

Sgula, you don't really have that many guys knocking on your door. Maybe this is not a bad idea after all.

Sgula

Hedva, I don't like him. What can I do about it?

Hedva

I see, but you shouldn't push him away so quickly.

Sgula

Hedva, I don't want him and that's the end of it.

Hedva

I see…and that's why he took you to show…

Sgula

Apparently.

Hedva

Well, the show's tonight. He won't bother you anymore.

Sgula

It's not just me. He bothers Danny, too.

Hedva

Danny?

Sgula

He's the bear.

Hedva

So?

Sgula

Ro'ee keeps picking on him.

Hedva

What do you mean picking?

Sgula

You know…he makes these remarks…

Hedva

That's what a director does, isn't it?

Sgula

Not these kinds of remarks.

Hedva

What do you mean "not these kinds"?

Sgula

Today we have our first dress rehearsal—but not Danny. He's had to wear the bear skin and mask for three days already, and it's such an uncomfortable costume. You can't—

Hedva

If it's so heavy and uncomfortable, he needs to get used to it, right?

Sgula

Maybe, but it's not only this. It's…

Hedva

What?

Sgula

You know what? Come and see for yourself what I mean.

Hedva

Why do you worry so much about Danny?

Sgula

> It was one of the terms I set when Ro'ee wanted me to be in the show. I wanted to bring Danny.

Hedva

> Why Danny?

Sgula

> He's cute. I thought we would have some fun, but now he's depressed because of the comments Ro'ee keeps making! Come to the rehearsal and help me calm Danny down.

Hedva

> What will Ro'ee say if I come?

Sgula

> I don't know what he'll say. Why should he care? You know what? I'll tell everybody at the rehearsal that you came because *I* invited you. Okay?

Hedva

> I don't know…

Sgula

> What's wrong with you? I know we were never really friends, and suddenly I'm coming to you with these questions, but you can trust me. What happened to you? You're so lost in your own thoughts…

Hedva

> Nothing happened.

Sgula

> The whole kibbutz makes preparations for children's day. Building an obstacle course, a merry go round, cleaning and decorating the yard at the kindergarten, putting on a play, and you're the only one who—

Hedva

> I'm helping decorate the dining hall for the holiday.

Sgula

> The holiday?

Hedva

> Sukkot! We decorate the dining hall to make it look like a Sukkah. Flowers on the walls, you know.

Sgula

> It's still a *week* until Sukkot! Hedva, what's the matter with you? What happened?

Hedva

> What happened to me can happen to any girl.

Sgula

> Meaning?

Hedva

> What happens sometimes…to a girl…a girl our age…

Sgula

> Are you sick?

Hedva

> No.

Sgula

> So?

Hedva

> I told you. It happens to everybody.

Sgula

> You've fallen in love?

Hedva

> Hasn't it ever happened to you?

Sgula

> So it's true…'cause I heard something. And who's the lucky guy?

Hedva

I've already said too much. Forget I mentioned it.

Sgula

I'm ready to forget, but you...
(The office door opens - Doobi, Zoltty, and Arnon, the secretary of the kibbutz, walk out of the office.)

Zoltty

Doobi, I don't think you understand the situation! What will happen here if everyone does what he want?

Doobi

And the guys in the orchard who sit there threatening the kibbutz? Do you think the kibbutz will really fall apart...

Arnon

Doobi...

Zoltty

You tell then! *You* go to the orchard and talk to them now! You tell them to come back home! Doobi, we can't afford strikes in the kibbutz! Who on earth are they striking against? The kibbutz doesn't belong to me! It's...

Doobi

But why me?

Zoltty

You are the head of the junior section in Ein Ro'eem, and most of them, out there in the orchard, are young people, so...

Arnon

That's right, Doobi. Most of them are young people. You have some responsibility.

Doobi

And what exactly am I supposed to tell them?

Zoltty

> Explain the situation. I don't think they really understand the situation.

Arnon

> Don't you agree that decisions should be respected?

Doobi

> All you're afraid of is that the people in the kibbutz will find out about the strike and will ask questions. That they'll want to know why the orchard workers are on strike.

Arnon

> What are you talking about?

Zoltty

> We're not afraid of any questions. The kibbutz meeting has already resulted in a decision. Part of the orchard is going to be cleared.

Doobi

> And I am the one…I am the one…

Zoltty

> You go and talk to them. You are the one. And I want to tell you this—if you don't go over there and talk to them, you risk everything you've achieved here in Ein Ro'eem. Head of the junior section, member of the Financial Board—you're jeopardizing everything!

Doobi

> Really!

Zoltty

> You just don't get it, do you?

Arnon

> There is no need to make threats…

Zoltty

> These strikes are very dangerous!

Hedva

    (To Sgula.)

    Did you hear that? Threats!

Sgula

    I heard.

Arnon

    Go, Doobi, have a word with them. Listen to Zoltty. He's the head of the Financial Board, and he knows what's best.

Doobi

    I'll go, but I'm not sure what I'm going to tell them.
    (Turns to leave.)

Hedva

    Doobi, what's the matter?

Doobi

    Nothing.

Hedva

    But what happened?

Doobi

    Nothing happened.
    (Leaves.)

Zoltty

    Talk with them, Doobi.
    (Zoltty and Arnon turn toward the head office.)

Hedva

    Zoltty, what happened? What are all those threats about?

Zoltty

    Ask Doobi. He will tell you.
    (Zoltty and Arnon enter the office.)

Hedva

> Did you hear what he said? All those threats?

Sgula

> I heard.

Hedva

> And Doobi has no parents in the kibbutz…so…

Sgula

> So what? Hedva, don't you worry about Doobi.

Hedva

> But he wants Doobi to leave the kibbutz? Or what?

Sgula

> Doobi? Leave? What's the matter with you, Hedva? Since when do you care so much about Doobi?

Hedva

> It's not just about Doobi. It's about all of us.
> *(Leaves.)*

Sgula

> Maybe he's the lucky one? Hedva, I hope he's not the one you…find someone else, but not Doobi.
> *(Leaves.)*

SCENE 2

Another place in the kibbutz. Doobi and Efroni are present.

Efroni

But why do you have to mess with such a—

Doobi

He asked me, so…

Efroni

Zoltty asked you…

Doobi

Yes he did…and…

Efroni

And you do whatever Zoltty asks you to do?

Doobi

I want to help…there's a strike…

Efroni

But it's in the orchard! What do you—

Doobi

I'm the head of the junior section, and most of the orchard workers…

Efroni

> But the problem has nothing to do with the young ones or the old ones! It's an economic problem!

Doobi

> I want to help. That's all. So…I'll talk to them…and…

Efroni

> But why you?

Doobi

> This is my kibbutz, and yours, and we have to do something.

Efroni

> Talk to them…really, Doobi, come on…

Doobi

> If you don't want to, just forget it, okay?

Efroni

> I'm working…you know…

Doobi

> I'm working too. You can work more after business hours are over.

Efroni

> But in the working hours? You're not going to find them now. Maybe in the evening.

Doobi

> In the evening? With flashlights?

Efroni

> In the evening they gather at their hut. Now they are working.

Doobi

> I'm sure we can find them now.

Efroni

> You will find them. I'm not going.

Doobi

> It won't take long. Twenty minutes, half an hour…not more.

Efroni

> I'm not going. I just don't know why you do this. Do you do it as a member of the Financial Board or as the head of the junior section?

Doobi

> Listen, do you want to help or not?

Efroni

> To help, yeah. But I'd like to know…

Doobi

> Do you want to or not?

Efroni

> I don't understand…

Doobi

> Forget it. Just forget it.
> *(Leaves.)*

Scene 3

In a field near the kibbutz. A small stage. There is a large board for decoration at the back of the stage. Next to the stage and backstage there is a set of drums and four chairs for the band. Ro'ee is the director, Danny is in a bear costume, Sgula is in a princess costume, and Shulamit, Amalia, and Irit are dressed as squirrels.

Sgula

> *(Holding the bear's paw.)*

> Come, my sweet bear. Let's go to your home. Show me where you live. I don't want to live in the palace. My daddy, the king, keeps telling me what to do, but I'm not a child! He tells me when to get up in the morning, when to eat, when to go to sleep. I don't like it. Children, do you like it? When people tell you what to do? Do you? Do you? I can't hear you.

Ro'ee

> Your hand! On your ear!
> *(Demonstrates the pose.)*

> You keep forgetting!

Sgula

> Yeah. Sorry.
> *(Puts her hand to her ear.)*

> Do you like it? When people tell you what to do? No, you don't. My daddy wants me to come to the king's council,

where they sit and chatter all the time. And after all that blabbering, Daddy does whatever he wants to do anyway. Come, my sweet bear. When I saw you wandering by the palace, I thought to myself that this bear will get me out of here. I'm so bored in the palace, and I heard that you have a lot of honey in your cave. I love sweet things, and in the palace I'm not allowed to eat any. This is forbidden, and that is forbidden. Do you have any honey?

Ro'ee

This is forbidden, and that is forbidden—show it with your hands—this…and that…show it! Show it!

Sgula

This is forbidden…that is forbidden…

Ro'ee

Good, good. Why are you laughing, Miss Amalia?

Amalia

I'm not…it's just—

Ro'ee

I don't know what makes you laugh, but this is the correct way to do it.
(To Sgula.)

Go on. Go on.

Sgula

I heard that you have honey in your cave. Do you? Do you?
(Danny in the bear costume growls. Amalia laughs.)

Ro'ee

Why are you growling? You have to nod! Growl *and* nod!
(Danny growls and nods.)

Good. Good. Even louder!

Sgula

Do you have honey?
(Danny nods and growls.)

Ro'ee

Good! The children will laugh!

Irit

It sounds scary.

Ro'ee

Scary…okay…let it be scary. Go on. You, in the forest now.

Sgula

Where is your cave? Is it far away? Come. Come. I can't see anything. The forest is too dense here.
(The girls in the squirrel costumes start to jump around.)

Come. You move so slowly, that the winter will come before we get there, you'll fall asleep, and we'll never reach your cave. Oh! Is that your cave?
(Danny nods and growls.)

Here we are! Come, my sweet bear! I see a lot of honey! Oh!
(Sits on the floor and pretends to eat honey.)

Don't you eat, my sweet bear?
(Danny sits and pretends to eat.)

Oh! I ate too much! I have a stomachache! My daddy always told me not to eat too much, and now I can't move!

Ro'ee

Now the orchestra, which hasn't arrived yet…

Shulamit

The band.

Ro'ee

The band, which hasn't arrived yet, starts to play a lullaby… and you fall asleep, put your head on his shoulder…right… and you can caress her head with your…palms…

Amalia

What happened to the band?

Ro'ee

> Yudke told me that neither he nor Ronen could make it on time, so I agreed that all four of them should come *(Looks at his watch.)*
>
> later.

Amalia

> You agreed, and they took advantage.

Ro'ee

> No. I agreed that we will do a special rehearsal with them. Later.

Irit

> Aren't we supposed to rehearse with them?

Ro'ee

> We will. We will. There's another rehearsal afternoon. Don't worry.

Shulamit

> Rehearsals aren't important. Let's hope that they'll be on time for the actual show.

Ro'ee

> They will. They will.

Amalia

> On the contrary—rehearsals are the important thing. Isn't what you said?

Ro'ee

> Rehearsals are the important thing?

Amalia

> Didn't you say so?

Ro'ee

> That's not what I said. I said—

Shulamit

> He said that whenever we do something, we're just rehearsing. A soldier, when shooting and shouting, is just rehearsing being a commander. A schoolboy, when he learns, is just rehearsing taking his exams.

Ro'ee

> That's not exactly what I said. The soldier rehearses the real battle, not being a commander. But this isn't important…

Shulamit

> Old people go to the synagogue, pray, consult with doctors, think about death…

Irit

> You remember everything…

Ro'ee

> That's what I said three years ago, when I was new to the kibbutz, and now, when show time is just around the corner, I can see what's important. Okay. We are in the jungle, the mighty jungle—you fall asleep…
> (*Hedva enters.*)
> You…

Sgula

> Hedva!

Ro'ee

> Hedva? What are you doing here?

Hedva

> I just…just…

Sgula

> I asked her to come. To help…to comment…

Ro'ee

> To comment on *what*?

Sgula

> On my…acting…

Ro'ee

> That's the reason *I* am here.

Hedva

> Who is the bear?
> *(Danny takes off his mask.)*
> Danny!

Sgula

> I told you!

Irit

> You should hear him roar! All the animals run away

Danny

> I can hardly can breathe with that mask on!

Irit

> But you roar all right!

Danny

> Yeah…roar…

Irit

> He doesn't like the role. He thinks that the role isn't really important.

Ro'ee

> It's a very important role. Great actors put on masks sometimes. Really. You can do many things with a mask on your face. Jump, move…

Shulamit

> He's a bear! He's supposed to be heavy!

Ro'ee

Yes, but he can show it…he can…act it out…

Irit

It's just a show for children! You do it…like…

Ro'ee

Even a show for children should be done right.

Amalia

You want him to be funny, you want him to be scary. He is just…

Ro'ee

Funny…yes. It's a comedy, after all.

Danny

Anyone can do it.

Ro'ee

Not anyone.

Danny

Anyone who can fit in the costume.

Ro'ee

Everyone…okay…back to the rehearsal.
(Looks in the script in his hand.)

You fall asleep…now we'll skip the scene in the palace, the king wonders where his daughter is…sends his messengers out into the forest…they'll come to the next rehearsal too…

Irit

You let them…you let them…

Ro'ee

I didn't let anybody anything! There are people who have to work, and they will be at the last rehearsal! Let's do as much as we can! Let's…

Hedva

(*Looking at the empty chairs.*)

What are those chairs doing here?

IRit

A band.

Hedva

A band...

Sgula

Yes. A band.

Irit

We haven't even seen them yet!

Shulamit

Let alone heard them...

Irit

But they will be on time. So Ro'ee says.

Ro'ee

Listen, there's a special rehearsal for the band, within an hour. And there *is* a rehearsal for all the actors—the general rehearsal—this afternoon. Okay? We finish now. We'll continue the rehearsal this afternoon, around four o'clock. That's it. You're free to go.

Irit

We're free?

Ro'ee

Yes. Until four o'clock. Be on time.
(*The three squirrels and Sgula go backstage to change. Danny takes the bear costume off. Ro'ee looks at the script.*)

Hedva

Danny, come on.

Danny

> What?

Hedva

> Come, come .
> *(To Ro'ee.)*
> I take Danny.

Ro'ee

> What do you mean?

Hedva

> I take him. Don't worry. We'll be back on time. Come on,
> Danny.

Danny

> Where are you taking me?

Hedva

> Come on, come on.

Danny

> Yeah, yeah, come on, come on…
> *(Hedva and Danny leave.)*

Ro'ee

> Be back on time!
> *(The three squirrels emerge from backstage after changing, Irit says
> "bye" and they turn to leave.)*

Ro'ee

> And tell the members of the band, if you see them, that I
> canceled the special rehearsal for them, and to come to the
> last rehearsal this afternoon. Okay?

Irit

> Okay.

Ro'ee

> We have to do a rehearsal together, and there's no reason for them to come now. And be on time!

Amalia

> We will.
> *(The squirrels leave. Sgula emerges from backstage after changing and starts to leave.)*

Ro'ee

> Sgula! Wait a minute!

Sgula

> What?

Ro'ee

> Wait.

Sgula

> Wait for what?

Ro'ee

> Wait for me. I want to go with you to the kibbutz.

Sgula

> Why?

Ro'ee

> I want to talk to you about your role.

Sgula

> My role…

Ro'ee

> And I want you to help me bring some stuff back here from the kibbutz.

Sgula

> But…I'm not going back to the kibbutz now.

Ro'ee

> You aren't?

Sgula

> No. I would like to take a walk and wander around. There are places that I haven't seen a long time.

Ro'ee

> And this is the time…to go…

Sgula

> Yes. Yes. We will talk later.
> *(Leaves.)*

Scene 4

In the orchard. The workers Kessler, Nathan, David, and Ramie are sitting around a table set to eat, making salad and spreading cheese on slices of bread for breakfast. The hut of the orchard is behind them.

Kessler

> The problem is patience. We cannot win without patience. Those who keep looking at their watches, who want a quick victory, accomplish nothing. I also hope we won't need to sit here much longer, but you guys don't have any patience. It won't work this way. You can't go on strike here for three days and then hope that everything'll work out. What's wrong with sleeping in sleeping bags? You were all in the army, warriors, weren't you?

David

> Not Nathan. In the army he worked in the canteen.

Nathan

> You would wish...you would wish...

Ramie

> Believe me, Kessler, sleeping here isn't the problem. We're all young...more or less...

David

> Except Efrayim. But he doesn't sleep here at night. He goes home in the afternoon.

Kessler

> That's right. By the way, where is he? Doesn't he want to eat breakfast?

David

> He'll be here later.

Kessler

> Have you seen him this morning?

David

> Yes, I've seen him. He'll be here.

Kessler

> Later.

Ramie

> Anyway, the nights aren't the problem. All of us, except you, are single. The problem is that I'm not sure anyone in the kibbutz knows about us. I mean, about us being on strike. That we're sitting here and not coming home in the afternoon. You think all the people in the kibbutz are talking about our strike, but…

David

> And even if they do know, do they really care?

Ramie

> That's another story. And maybe it's true. Maybe nobody really cares. But I still think that no one even knows about us.

Kessler

> I'm sure that there are people who know, and care.

Ramie

Who knows?

Kessler

I don't know exactly who, but I'm sure someone knows, and whoever doesn't know yet will know within few days—if we're still here. And then people will ask questions - why are they on strike? What happened? Why—

Ramie

They'll also ask why we're here.

Kessler

No...

Ramie

Yes, they will. The decision was to clear part of the orchard, and you sit there—

Kessler

No. They know we're good workers and good kibbutzniks. They know...

David

They'll say if we're such good kibbutzniks, come home and speak at the kibbutz meeting. Don't...

Nathan

And nobody wants to stand against Zoltty. Zoltty said so—it's okay.

Kessler

No...no.

Ramie

Yes, yes.

Kessler

I say, if we'll stay here, something will happen! People will talk about our strike.

David

> And then what?

Kessler

> Then we'll see. Don't give up so fast! Don't—

Ramie

> I still think no one knows.

David

> Ramie is right. When you will return to the kibbutz and run into one of the members in the dining room, he'll say…

Kessler

> What up with this saltshaker? It's not empty, but nothing gets out.

Nathan

> It's the humidity. We should put rice in it.

David

> He'll say, "Kessler! Where've you been? I haven't seen you in such a long time! Have you been abroad? Or, god forbid, have you been ill?" "No," you'll say, "I was in the orchard, on strike." "On strike? What do you mean on strike?" And when you'll begin to explain, you'll find out that he never heard about the decision to clear part of the orchard—let alone about our strike!

KessLer

> So he doesn't know. But there are people who know.

Ramie

> But who?

Kessler

> I don't know. But I'm sure—

David

> And your friend in the dining room will tell you, "Good for you! Go on with your strike! Good luck to you!" And then he'll go on with his day.

Kessler

> And what will people say if we go back after only three days? "Are they afraid?"

Ramie

> No one will say anything, 'cause no one knows.

David

> And what will people say if we go back after two week? After all, we have to go back sometime.

Kessler

> Yeah, but something will happen!

Nathan

> Or it won't.

David

> How long will we have to sit here?

Kessler

> What do you want me to say?

David

> I'm just asking…

Kessler

> How should I know?

David

> Days, weeks…

Kessler

> Of course days. Not weeks.

David

> Days…

Nathan

> The truth is…the truth is…

Ramie

> *(Pointing to Nathan's plate.)*

> Look. Look. He's eating. Look, within a day or two we'll run out of food, and he's eating.

Kessler

> What wrong?

Ramie

> Look…

Kessler

> Listen, people don't like how Zoltty is acting. So—

David

> They don't like it, but who cares?

Nathan

> How Zoltty acts…how Zoltty acts…

Ramie

> Kessler, what does your wife say?

Kessler

> She doesn't love it. Not at all.

Ramie

> She doesn't…

Kessler

> She doesn't like that I'm staying here…it's been three days.

Nathan

> And three nights...

Kessler

> We have a little kid…and…but she understands.

David

> Understands what?

Kessler

> The situation.
> *(Suzan appears from inside the hut, wearing an apron, holding a big pan, walking between them to serve each person a piece of an omelet.)*

Nathan

> Thanks, Suzan.

Kessler

> Have you eaten yet, Suzan?

Suzan

> Yes, I have.
> *(Finishes serving the omelet and goes back into the hut. The four men start eating.)*

Ramie

> Does she tell people about our strike?

Kessler

> I don't know. It's not easy for her, you know. What about Efrayim? Where is he? David, you said you saw him this morning, didn't you?

David

> Yes, I did.

Kessler

> Where is he?

David

> I don't know. Working.

Kessler

Suzan wants to clean, wash the dishes, and he shows up late, tells stories, eats slowly…

Ramie

Maybe he can tell people about the strike. He goes back home every day. He can—

David

I don't know if he can.

Ramie

Why not?

David

He doesn't talk! He only mumbles!

Nathan

When he's busy doing something, he forgets about everything else.

David

I saw him talking to a leaky *faucet*! Talking to it! His job is to fix it, not talk to it.

Ramie

But can't he tell people?

David

He can't talk! He just mumbles! Mumbles! No words! Nobody understands him!

Kessler

We don't need Efrayim! We…
(Suzan comes out of the hut without her apron, holding a coffee pot, and sets it on the table.)

Suzan

Leave the dishes. I'll clean up when I get back.
(Leaves.)

Ramie

> Where's she going?

Kessler

> I don't know.

Nathan

> What do you care where's she is going? As long as she cooks, cleans…

Ramie

> I don't care. I just want to know.

Kessler

> She's doing her job all right. So, what do you say? Are we staying here?

Ramie

> Stay here? But the question is for how long.

Kessler

> We'll talk about it every day in the morning. Okay?

Ramie

> Staying…

Nathan

> Speaking of the ways Zoltty has been acting, I would like to say that thanks to his actions we got the spray gun.

Ramie

> What spray gun?

Nathan

> The yellow one.

Ramie

> What yellow one?

Kessler

It's not yellow anymore. It's all covered in rust now. We don't use it anymore. So, are we staying or not?

David

Staying. Staying.

Ramie

For today. We'll see about tomorrow.

SCENE 5

In the orchard. Hedva and Danny are sitting under a tree.

Hedva

      I just wanna know what Ro'ee…

Danny

      I told you…and…

Hedva

      But what did he do? What did he say?

Danny

      He wants Sgula…how can I say it…you can see it in the way he acts around her…by his—

Hedva

      Yes, but what do you mean the way he acts? What did he say? What did he do?

Danny

      He said…I don't know…Hedva, what do you want from me? I don't remember. He said this…he said that…

Hedva

      You were in the rehearsals for more than a *month,* and you don't remember what the director said?

Danny

      How can I remember everything? How—

Hedva

> Not everything. But you can see, you can…

Danny

> Why is it so important to you to know what he said?

Hedva

> It's not important. It's interesting.

Danny

> Interesting…

Hedva

> The education board of the kibbutz appointed me to deal with it. Okay?

Danny

> The education board? Hedva, you…

Hedva

> What's the matter with you, Danny? What did I ask you? I just asked…

Danny

> But I don't know what to tell you!

Hedva

> You can…you can try…

Danny

> I didn't know that this kind of gossip interests you.

Hedva

> It doesn't interest me so much, but since we were walking here together, you can tell me.

Danny

> We're walking together because you took me out of the rehearsal. I didn't know it was for this kind of gossip. If I'd known…

Hedva

It's not gossip. It's something that's important to know.

Danny

Important…

Hedva

Maybe I can help.

Danny

Help? Help whom?

Hedva

I can give advice.

Danny

Give advices to whom? Who's—

Hedva

To whoever needs it. Danny, what's going on with you? Why are you so negative? I've always been your best friend. So why…

Danny

I don't remember you being my best friend.

Hedva

You forgot. Never mind. Come and help me to look for green branches to decorate the kibbutz dining room. At least…

Danny

Decorate? Why?

Hedva

Sukkot! The holiday! Danny, what's wrong with you? Don't you know *anything, anything* at all?

Danny

I got a part in the show!

Hedva

> The show…very nice…but for now you can help me. It won't do you any harm to contribute something…

Danny

> I won't carry dry branches to the dining room now! Hedva, what do you—

Hedva

> After all I've done for you…after all I've done for you…

Danny

> What have you done for me? What have you…

Hedva

> You forgot everything. You forgot everything.

Danny

> I don't remember that you…

Hedva

> Come on, come here. I'll give you a kiss.

Danny

> No. No.

Hedva

> Come here.

Danny

> Leave me alone.
>
> *(Leaves.)*

Scene 6

In the orchard, Efrayim, and Shlomo, holding a knife and a few bamboo canes in his hands.

Efrayim

> I realize that all you want is to build a sukkah by your house, but you can't cut bamboo without permission.

Shlomo

> Why do I need permission? It's growing wild, isn't it?

Efrayim

> No. We planted it, to protect the trees. Without the bamboo, the trees would be damaged by the wind and the hail. At least the trees along the border. The wind shakes the trees, branches break, and fruit drops.

Shlomo

> You're afraid of the wind...

Efrayim

> Afraid, no...but you gotta see the wind here in the winter. I'm telling you, it's really something—it damages the trees, it damages everything...the fruit...

Shlomo

> Don't be afraid. If the roots are strong, everything is strong.

Efrayim

> Not the roots…the branches…the fruit…

Shlomo

> How much did I take? Look—it's not so much.

Efrayim

> Everyone will come and take some, and take some…

Shlomo

> No one will come. Have you seen anybody except me?

Efrayim

> I don't know…

Shlomo

> I took a cane here, a cane there, so it doesn't affect—

Efrayim

> Are you from Bait Anan?

Shlomo

> Yes, I'm from Bait Anan.

Efrayim

> People will see you and will do what you have done.

Shlomo

> No one will see me—no one looks at me. No one cares. Believe me. Everyone has boards. One took them from here, one took them from there. There isn't anything left for me, so I came here. What's your name?

Efrayim

> Efrayim.

Shlomo

> Efrayim. My name is Shlomo. Do you want me to put these back? I can't put these canes back, can I?

Efrayim

No, you can't.

Shlomo

I could try to replant them…

Efrayim

It's really difficult to replant bamboo. It's difficult…as difficult as…

Shlomo

Yes. Do you know, Mr. Efrayim, what's written in the Bible about this holiday?

Efrayim

This holiday?

Shlomo

Yes! Sukkot! "Thou shalt dwell in sukkah seven days." Did you build a sukkah, Mr. Efrayim?

Efrayim

No. In the kibbutz we decorate the dining hall like a green sukkah, with ornaments, green branches, flowers…so…

Shlomo

That's good! That's good! At least you do something! And do you know…

Efrayim

But it's also written that "thou shalt not steal." Did you know that?

Shlomo

No no no! Don't say that! Don't say such a thing, Mr. Efrayim! God forbid! Don't even…

Efrayim

I'm just saying…I'm just saying.

Shlomo

> And you received a lot of land from the government. You got a lot of…of—

Efrayim

> But today it's very hard to make a living from the land. Believe me, Mr. Shlomo.

Shlomo

> You can't make a living as a farmer?

Efrayim

> Barely…barely. Believe me.

Shlomo

> But I can see that you're doing well…I can see…

Efrayim

> No, no…we have debts…

Shlomo

> You're doing fine…I can tell. You complain, but you're doing fine.

Efrayim

> No, we aren't. Have you heard about the price gap?

Shlomo

> Price what?

Efrayim

> The price gap. You buy an orange in the market, right? You pay, but hardly any of that money finds its way to us. There are drivers, merchants, shopkeepers…everybody takes his part, so…

Shlomo

> So nothing is left for you…I see…

Efrayim

>Almost nothing.

Shlomo

>So why don't you sell your merchandise on the side of the road?

Efrayim

>It's forbidden.

Shlomo

>Forbidden? Why?

Efrayim

>It's against the law.

Shlomo

>Against the law?

Efrayim

>That's right. If you sell something on the side of the road, a policeman will come and give you a fine. A very big fine.

Shlomo

>A fine?

Efrayim

>A very big fine. Do you know what a big fine is? It's...it's...

Shlomo

>Okay, okay, I see. But how many canes have I taken, really? Look. How many? One. Two. Three...

Efrayim

>Okay...

Shlomo

>Four...five...

Efrayim

    Okay, but…

Shlomo

    Believe me, I hardly took anything at all.
    (Leaves)

Scene 7

The small stage near the kibbutz. Yudke, Ronen, Avner, and Eli, the band members who are participating in the show, are sitting with their instruments. Eli is seated at the drum set.

Ronen

How long are we gonna wait here?

Yudke

Let's wait
(Looks at his watch.)
a little bit more.

Ronen

Then what?

Yudke

Then we'll see and make a decision. I think we got here on time.

Avner

Must be a misunderstanding.

Ronen

A misunderstanding on which side?

Avner

On both sides.

Yudke

Let's wait a little bit longer, and then…

Ronen

We showed up, with our instruments, but no one cares.

Yudke

What makes you say that? It's just a misunderstanding, that's all.

Eli

Ronen is right. No one cares. We play in the holidays, in weddings and celebrations, yet nobody appreciates what we do.

Yudke

Nobody appreciates us? Really, now…

Eli

I'm telling you! No one cares!

Yudke

What do you want people to do? Applaud more?

Eli

To…appreciate…

Yudke

But what do you want people to do?

Eli

I don't know…

Yudke

So let's sit here and cry…no one appreciates us…

Eli

Not cry…but…

Avner

Are you guys playing much together?

Ronen

> We're playing, you know, here and there.

Avner

> Here…there…

Yudke

> Don't worry. You won't have to play too much.

Eli

> Just when the board asks you to. That's all.

Avner

> Meaning?

Ronen

> Holidays…parties…

Eli

> At the end of the school year…at the beginning of the school year…

Yudke

> Since when is there a celebration at the end of the school year? Maybe the kids do something in their class, but…

Ronen

> There is! There are! I remember one, it was in the evening, by the swimming pool, on the lawn.

Eli

> That's right. I remember, too.

Yudke

> And we played there?

Ronen

> Yeah, we did. Maybe you weren't there. But we played.

Eli

There was a song that all the kids sang—I don't remember every word, but I remember the end. Our slogan is: Work and Learn.

Yudke

I do remember something like that, but I don't remember playing there.

Ronen

We did play there.

Eli

We played off key…

Ronen

Well, we do that no matter where we're playing, so…

Yudke

That's what *you* do, not me.

Eli

You weren't there, so…

Yudke

But I was.

Avner

Who's that walking over there?

Eli

I think it's Rafi.

Ronen

Hey! Hey! Rafi! Rafi! Come here! Rafi! Come!

Eli

Did he skip school or what?

Ronen

> They're not in school today. They're helping with the preparations for children's day. Rafi! Come here!
> (*Rafi, a young boy, enters.*)

Eli

> Rafi! What's up with you? Shouldn't you be in school?

Rafi

> No. We're working.

Yudke

> And where are you working?

Rafi

> In banana land.

Ronen

> Banana land?

Rafi

> Yeah.

Eli

> That's what Soly Cohen calls the plantation.

Avner

> Aren't you helping with the preparations for children's day?

Rafi

> No. Several students are helping, but most of us are working as usual.

Yudke

> Working?

Avner

> When you were walking over here, did you happen to see Ro'ee?

Ronen

> The great, awful director?

Rafi

> No. No.

Avner

> And why are you going to work at this hour? Aren't you little late?

Rafi

> They didn't wake me up.

Avner

> Who was supposed to wake you up?

Rafi

> I don't know, but he didn't wake me.

Ronen

> Can't you think of a better excuse than that? Just…

Rafi

> I can't think of anything, okay?
> *(Leaves.)*

Yudke

> Buy an alarm clock!

Avner

> He doesn't have any money. Do you know…

Eli

> His parents do, I think.

Ronen

> He doesn't need an alarm clock. There's someone who's responsible for waking them up every morning, but sometimes they don't get up. Not just to the work, but for school, too.

Eli

>Our slogan, work and learn…

Avner

>Late or not late—they *are* working - we are not…

Ronen

>My boss didn't like the fact that I'm going to rehearsal in middle of the day.

Yudke

>Don't you worry, I'll talk to your boss.

Eli

>Working or not—we're not rehearsing either.

Ronen

>This isn't our fault.

Eli

>I'm not so sure…

Yudke

>Let's play!

Eli

>But we did play! We have to do it with the actors!

Yudke

>That's all we can do now.
>*(Ro'ee enters, carrying plastic bags.)*
>What's going on, Ro'ee?

Ro'ee

>You shouldn't come.

Yudke

>Why not?

Avner

>There's no rehearsal?

Ro'ee

> There was a rehearsal, but it ended earlier than we thought it would. And you were late…

Yudke

> We told you we were going to be late!

Ro'ee

> You're okay. You told me. But it was over earlier than we thought, so we decided to go home. Didn't you run into the girls?

Eli

> What girls?

Ro'ee

> The girls! The squirrels! I asked them to tell you to go home and to come later this afternoon for the final rehearsal. Didn't you see them?

Avner

> No.

Yudke

> No.

Eli

> They must've taken a shortcut to get to the kibbutz. So…

Ronen

> The donkey path.

Ro'ee

> Perhaps you should be taking this path too…but never mind…

Eli

> We aren't donkeys…

Ro'ee

> Anyway, it's not your fault.

Eli

Not our fault…

Ro'ee

Not at all! And I want to tell you, I've only lived in the kibbutz for three years, but I've noticed you guys, and I'm very impressed with your persistence and your consistency. You show through your music that there's some culture in this place. But you guys play…play…
(Puts the plastic bags down near the stage and turns to leave.)

Yudke

Where are you going?

Ro'ee

We'll meet in the afternoon at the final rehearsal. See you. At four. Four thirty at the latest.

Eli

What are you running around for? Come on, sit down, take it easy.

Ro'ee

Play, play.
(Leaves.)

Ronen

So he's noticed us.

Yudke

Let's play.

Eli

Did you hear what he said about the power of music?

Yudke

What he said about the power of music?

Eli

Didn't you hear what he said?

Yudke

No. I didn't.

Eli

Music gives us wings…only music…only music…changes the mood…

Ronen

Hey, hey, I don't want to hear his lectures.

Eli

No, listen to this. He said—

Ronen

He said…

Avner

When he first came to the kibbutz he used to say things like that, but people didn't think that what he had to say was very clever, so he stopped…

Yudke

They're wrong to think that way about him—he said some nice things too. Let's play that part when…you know, from the beginning of the play. I hope that this time we play in tune.

(The band starts to play.)

Scene 8

In the orchard. Doobi, Kessler.

Doobi

> Kessler, you can't just sit here and not go to the meeting, and—

Kessler

> We aren't just sitting here. We're on strike.

Doobi

> On strike...you're just ignoring the decisions that were made during the last meeting.

Kessler

> You know that Zoltty rules the meeting. Everybody listens to him. Nobody dares speak out...

Doobi

> Did you attend that meeting?

Kessler

> That meeting? About the orchard?

Doobi

> Yes.

Kessler

> Yes, I attended that meeting.

Doobi

> And did you speak?

Kessler

> Yes, I spoke.

Doobi

> I don't remember hearing you speak…

Kessler

> Sure, I spoke. I don't know what you were doing during the meeting…

Doobi

> What was I doing? I was listening.

Kessler

> So you should have heard me.

Doobi

> If you spoke, I heard you, but I don't remember everything.

Kessler

> I spoke, but talk is useless. No one…

Doobi

> The question is, what did you say? Maybe…

Kessler

> It doesn't matter what I said. People didn't listen.

Doobi

> People listened. I'm sure.

Kessler

> They listened, but only to Zoltty.

Doobi

> Forget about Zoltty. You're always—

Kessler

But Zoltty makes all the decisions! For the Financial Board, and in the meetings!

Doobi

You can always appeal the decision.

Kessler

Appeal?

Doobi

Yes. Appeal the decision made in the meeting. About the orchard.

Kessler

And what are the chances…

Doobi

Kessler, you have to try!

Kessler

Try…

Doobi

Do you know that people who didn't attend the meeting can appeal the decision that was made there? Did you know that?

Kessler

As far as I know, you have to appeal within a week, and it's already been a month!

Doobi

Not within a week…it's two weeks. But we'll talk to the secretary. We're dealing with special circumstances here. I think—

Kessler

You mean talk to Arnon?

Doobi

Yes! The secretary! But you have to go back! Did all the orchard workers attend that meeting?

Kessler

I don't know. And if we appeal, what would we say? Zoltty…

Doobi

You have to persuade people. Make your own calculations. You say that there's no reason to clear the orchard, so you have to talk—and I will help you.

Kessler

You will help…

Doobi

Yes, I will! And don't you forget, I'm a member of the Financial Board! I can help…

Kessler

I'm glad that you want to help, but the question is…

Doobi

Of all the orchard workers, who was not at the meeting?

Kessler

I don't know. I think we all were at the meeting.

Doobi

Nathan? Efrayim?

Kessler

As far as I can remember, they were there.

Doobi

Is Gady Sofer working with you?

Kessler

No…no…

Doobi

> You have to find someone who didn't attend the meeting.

Kessler

> Come on, Doobi.

Doobi

> Why not?

Kessler

> Seriously…

Doobi

> Kessler, do something! You can't just sit here and complain.
> *(Ramie enters.)*
>
> Hello, Ramie. How are you?

Ramie

> Fine, just fine.

Doobi

> Did you go to the meeting?

Ramie

> What meeting?

Doobi

> The meeting about the orchard.

Ramie

> I was there. Why?

Doobi

> Kessler will tell you. Okay. I'm going. I hope you will make
> the right decision.
> *(Turns to leave.)*

Kessler

> Where are you going? The kibbutz is over there.

Doobi

> I'm not going home now. I'm going to the bananas plantation.

Kessler

> The bananas…

Doobi

> Yes. Some of us in the mechanic's workshop made a device that supports their long sprinklers, and lately they've been complaining that something is wrong. That it doesn't work well. So this is a good opportunity to see what's all the noise is about. See ya!
> *(Leaves.)*

Ramie

> What is Doobi doing here?

Kessler

> He wants us to end the strike and come home.

Ramie

> To end the strike…

Kessler

> He said that we can appeal the decision that was made at the meeting. He says anyone who didn't attend the meeting can appeal. That's why he asked you…

Ramie

> I was there!

Kessler

> And in order to appeal, we have to go home.

Ramie

> And what would happen if we would appeal?

Kessler

> I don't know…

Ramie

What does Doobi have to do with our strike?

Kessler

He says he wants to help.

Ramie

Help...

Kessler

So he says.

Ramie

Did Zoltty send him?

Kessler

I don't know.

Ramie

And even if he really does want to help, what could he do?

Kessler

How would I know...

Ramie

I think we should go home. Believe me, Kessler...

Kessler

We will talk about it later.

Ramie

We will talk…

Kessler

We will talk about it tonight.
(*Leaves.*)

SCENE 9

In the field. Danny and Lea.

Lea

> Are you from the kibbutz?

Danny

> Yes, I'm from the kibbutz.

Lea

> Ein Ro'eem?

Danny

> Yes. Ein Ro'eem.

Lea

> There are so many kibbutzim around here. You're from Ein Ro'eem?

Danny

> Yes, I am.

Lea

> So you must know where there are bamboo canes?

Danny

> There are some by the orchard...by the bananas...the avocados...

Lea

> Where's the closest place I can find them?

Danny

> In the orchard, I think. Why?

Lea

> You think…you're from the kibbutz…you must know where to find it…

Danny

> I don't work there.

Lea

> You don't work where?

Danny

> In the orchard.

Lea

> But you are from the kibbutz. You must know something…

Danny

> I think that I know. Why do you need bamboo?

Lea

> My dad went to look for bamboo canes, to build a green sukkah for Sukkot. So he went to the fields around the kibbutz, to find some canes. Mom sent us to help him—he's not young anymore…

Danny

> Us? Who's "us"?

Lea

> Me and my little brother. Mom asked us to help him. He wanted to build a sukkah …so…

Danny

> A sukkah? With canes? Why canes? What about boards? You know the song—we took a hammer, a nail, and boards together…

Lea

> That's just the way he builds a sukkah . I don't know. So she sent us to help him, because we were just getting in her way in the house. It's a holiday today and we don't have to go to school. So…

Danny

> Where are you from?

Lea

> Bait Anan.

Danny

> And where is your brother?

Lea

> My brother is from Bain Anan too, of course.

Danny

> No, I mean, where is he now?

Lea

> Gone!

Danny

> Gone?

Lea

> We started to go, my little brother and I, and he lagged behind. "I can't walk! You walk too fast!" Suddenly, when I looked back, he was gone!

Danny

> Gone?

Lea

> That's right! Gone!

Danny

> So he left you all alone.

Lea

> He won't get away with it, I can tell you. Not this time. Don't you worry. When I get home…

Danny

> I'm not worried about it, but you, alone, far away from home…

Lea

> I didn't know what to do. Should I wait for him? Keep going? Head back? Go home? And then I saw you. So I decided to ask you. Maybe you can help me.

Danny

> I'll help you. A pretty girl like you…

Lea

> Pretty girl…sure…

Danny

> No, I mean it! What's your name?

Lea

> Lea.

Danny

> Lea. I'm Danny. Are all the girls in Bait Anan so pretty?

Lea

> Yeah, right…pretty. You guys from the kibbutz, the way you talk…I know how it goes.

Danny

> Not me. I…

Lea

You're always sitting in the kibbutz, never getting out... never coming to see us...

Danny

I will come...I will...

Lea

You guys always talk very nice, but we never see you. We see you only from a distance. We see the kibbutz, not the people.

Danny

What do you mean from a distance?

Lea

We see your houses, but not the people.

Danny

I see...

Lea

Maybe we should go up this hill and look there?

Danny

Why this hill?

Lea

From the hill we'll have a better view, right?

Danny

No...no...it won't do you any good to go up there.

Lea

Okay, I guess you must know.
(They leave.)

SCENE 10

In the field near the kibbutz. Suzan, holding a bunch of flowers, and Sgula.

Sgula

>   Didn't anyone ever tell you not to pick flowers?

Suzan

>   No. No one's ever told me not to. But why not pick them? What…

Sgula

>   It's forbidden. There's a law against it.

Suzan

>   A law? A real law?

Sgula

>   Yes. A law.

Suzan

>   I didn't know that. Do they punish anyone who picks flowers?

Sgula

>   Sometimes they do. These are protected flowers. Enjoy but don't destroy.

Suzan

>   Protected?

Sgula

> Those
> *(Points to the flowers Suzan is holding.)*
>
> aren't protected anymore…

Suzan

> Next time I'll know better. All I wanted to do with them is decorate the hut in the orchard. They're not for me.

Sgula

> It doesn't matter who they're for. What would happen if everyone picked flowers in the field? If a ranger sees you, maybe he'll file a complaint against you at the police office.

Suzan

> Really?

Sgula

> Yes. Yes.

Suzan

> Are there a lot of rangers around here?

Sgula

> No. No. If you go straight to the hut now, the chances that you'll see one are very small. But don't do it again.

Suzan

> I see…

Sgula

> In America, isn't there a law against picking flowers?

Suzan

> I don't know…maybe special flowers. But these are not so special. What's that over there?

Sgula

> Where?

Suzan

> There.

Sgula

> That's Kibbutz Rosh Ha'Nikra.

Suzan

> Ah…

Sgula

> Those trees over there are part of the kibbutz, but you can't see the houses, because…

Suzan

> Will you come and help me decorate the hut of the orchard? It's not far away.

Sgula

> I don't know. I have to…I have…

Suzan

> Come and help me, just a little bit.

Sgula

> Do you want me to be an accomplice to your crime?

Suzan

> No. I wanted you to help me. That's all.

Sgula

> You just want to ensure you're not the only one involved in this crime…

Suzan

> No…no, that's not it.
> (*Leave.*)

Scene 11

In the orchard. David and Hedva.

David

> I don't understand. Did you hear about our strike or not?

Hedva

> I heard…I heard…

David

> What did you hear?

Hedva

> I heard that you're on strike because they're going to clear part of the orchard.

David

> When did you hear about our strike?

Hedva

> This morning.

David

> Where? Who told you?

Hedva

> I was near the head office and I heard people talking about it.

David

What did they say?

Hedva

I didn't really hear everything. I just was passing by, so…. What do you want from me, David?

David

I want to know if people know about our strike. That's all.

Hedva

I don't know if they know…

David

When you get back to the kibbutz, why don't you tell people about our strike? Not everyone knows.

Hedva

Not everyone…but…

David

So tell them. Tell them.

Hedva

Okay. Is Doobi here?

David

Doobi was here. Why do you ask?

Hedva

I thought I saw him here. What was he doing in the orchard?

David

He wanted to talk with the workers about the strike.

Hedva

Talk to the workers...

David

Yes.

Hedva

> Did he go back to the kibbutz?

David

> I don't know. I didn't see him. The guys told me.

got Hedva

> So he's back…

David

> I suppose so. Why are you so interested in Doobi?

Hedva

> It's just…I saw him, and I wanted to know what was he doing here…

David

> Hedva, I'm not sure Doobi is for you.

Hedva

> Doobi…isn't for me…

David

> He's not for you. That's what I say.

Hedva

> So he's not for me. What do you care if he's for me or not?

David

> I don't care, but…

Hedva

> For me…not for me…. who cares…

David

> Nobody cares. Forget it. Tell me—

Hedva

> You don't care, so I'm looking for Doobi. That's all.

David

I do care. Sure I do. But that's not what's important right now. What's important right now is the orchard. So I'm asking you…

Hedva

The truth is…you don't care…

David

Forget it, Hedva! Who cares, who doesn't care. There are more important things now! There are things…

Hedva

What do you want from me, David? I just came here to gather green branches to decorate the kibbutz dining room, so what—

David

What branches?

Hedva

Branches to decorate the dining room! For the holiday!

David

Do you want to take branches from the trees?

Hedva

Yes.

David

You're really going to do it…

Hedva

What's wrong with that?

David

Are you going to break branches from the trees? Do you know how much damage you are going to cause? Hedva, I just don't know what to say! You're oblivious to the consequence of your actions! I just…I just…we have enough troubles without this, and now you're here, trying to break…

Hedva

Gathering a few branches is really such a huge deal? What's wrong with you, David?

David

It can cause serious damage, doing something like that…

Hedva

So I won't gather any branches here. Okay?

David

Hedva, be serious, for once!

Hedva

I am serious. What do you want?

David

Do something useful.

Hedva

Useful...

David

That's right! Something useful for the kibbutz! Why not? Just once!

Hedva

I'm doing many useful things.

David

There are more important things than branches…really, decorating with green…come on, be serious.

Hedva

Okay…okay…
(Leave.)

Scene 12

In the orchard. Efrayim and Mahamid.

Mahamid

This isn't Kibbutz Kabry's orchard, is it?

Efrayim

No. This is Kibbutz Ein Ro'eem's orchard. Kabry's orchard is in that direction.

Mahamid

I walked in that direction…

Efrayim

Keep going. It's just a little further.

Mahamid

This looks just like Kabry's orchard.

Efrayim

Of course it looks like it. What do you expect?

Mahamid

I used to work in Kabry's orchard.

Efrayim

You used—

Mahamid

Yes. They fired me, but they didn't give me my last paycheck. The manager of the orchard said I had to come and get it. I haven't worked there in three months, and now I can't remember exactly how to get to their orchard anymore. Could you give me some water? I've walked so much, and I'm very thirsty.

Efrayim

I'll give you water. I can't give you oranges, 'cause they're not ripe yet.

Mahamid

I didn't ask oranges. Just water.

Efrayim

I know. I'm just saying, the oranges aren't ripe.

Mahamid

Sour.

Efrayim

They're hard. Immature. Do you know what immature means?

Mahamid

It means you can't eat them.

Efrayim

To eat them now would be like eating lemons. They'll hurt your teeth. You know what they say—the fathers have eaten sour grapes, and the children's teeth are set on edge.

Mahamid

Set on edge?

Efrayim

You know, the father eats the fruit and the children's teeth are affected.

Mahamid

> The fathers eat immature fruit, and it affects their kids? Why?

Efrayim

> It's a proverb. From the Bible. The fathers have eaten sour grapes, and the children's teeth are set on edge? It's a question.

Mahamid

> Ah…a question…

Efrayim

> Yes.

Mahamid

> And what is the answer?

Efrayim

> There is no answer…

Mahamid

> We say - don't treat the son badly just because you hate his father.

Efrayim

> Right. Let's go look for water. Where can we find some… where…

Mahamid

> I see a pipe over here.

Efrayim

> Not all pipes carry water around here. Some are completely dry. Let's look…look for…

Mahamid

> Why isn't there any water in the pipes here? Didn't you pay for the water?

Efrayim

No…it has nothing to do with whether we paid or not. It just that…that…

Mahamid

I know, there are pipes in our village. Sometimes there we don't have water in them either. People say that when there was a well in the village, it was better. There was always water in the well.

Efrayim

So, if there isn't any water in the pipes, you can go to the well.

Mahamid

No, they closed off the well with a fence. They were afraid children would fall in.

Efrayim

Where are you from?

Mahamid

Aramshe. People say it's a shame that they closed off the well. There was always water in the well…

Efrayim

The well belongs to the past. Let's…

Mahamid

But when we had a well in the village, it was a very good time for us. So they say…

Efrayim

But you're talking about something that's totally ancient! The well, it's an ancient thing!

Mahamid

No, you don't understand. You don't…

Efrayim

> What don't I understand?

Mahamid

> The well was a place where people—especially women—
> would meet, talk, you know, gossip, spread rumors about
> what happened here, what happened there…husbands,
> wives, boys, girls…you know. What goes on in an Arab
> village. That was the place where…

Efrayim

> Yes, but it belongs to the past. Let's look for some water for
> you.
> *(Leave.)*

SCENE 13

In the field. Danny and Lea.

Danny

> It was really nice with all the kids when we were children. At night we used to put four beds together, spread out the blankets…

Lea

> Why four?

Danny

> 'Cause there were four beds in every room. So we put them together, spread out the blankets on the floor under the beds, and crawled underneath. It was always lots of fun after lights out. We used to have pillows fight.

Lea

> Did all the children like it?

Danny

> I don't know…

Lea

> And what if someone is sick?

Danny

> He sleeps in a different room, so he doesn't get anyone else sick.

———

Lea

And his mother? Where was she when he was sick?

Danny

She would be sitting by his bed every evening, and after that she'd home. In the morning she'd come back if he was still sick. Every day though we'd all go to our parents' houses in the afternoon.

Lea

And in the evenings you'd go back to the children's dorm…

Danny

Yes, but let me tell you—there are young couples in the kibbutz who want their children at home, not in the dorm. I think they're worried for themselves, not for their children.

Lea

You used to have a good time, in the dorm…

Danny

Yes.

Lea

Your parents would go away, and you'd start…start…

Danny

That's right.
(*Yoske and Gershon enter.*)

Yoske

Are you from Ein Ro'eem? I think I saw you once…

Danny

I'm from Ein Ro'eem. She's from Bait Anan. Where are you from?

Gershon

Bait Anan?

Danny

Yes.

Yoske

We're from Kfar Me'eer. I think I saw you working in the banana plantation.

Danny

Yes. I used to work there. And the—

Gershon

You used to?

Danny

Yes. And the knives in your belts tell me that you work in the banana planation too.

Yoske

Yes. Tell me, what sort of celebration are you having today?

Danny

Celebration?

Yoske

We saw a group of children in the field—we figured they must be from your kibbutz—and there were three adults with them. One of them was playing the trombone. The children were wearing colorful hats. It seemed to us like a celebration, but not Sukkot…

Danny

Ah! Children's day!

Yoske

What's that?

Danny

Children's day. It happens once a year.

Yoske

Children's day…

Danny

> Don't you celebrate, once a year, the retarded children's day?

Yoske

> Our children are not retarded….But tell me – what's your name?

Danny

> Danny. She's Lea.

Yoske

> Danny. Tell me…

Danny

> She's Lea.

Yoske

> How do you do, Lea. Tell me, Danny, aren't there a lot of holidays during this time of year? Why would you want to add another one? Rosh Hashanah, Yom Kippur…

Danny

> Don't ask me. I didn't do it.

Gershon

> You guys say, one holiday more, one holiday less, what's the difference…

Lea

> They do love holidays.

Yoske

> And what kind of holiday is it? What do you do, other than what we saw?

Danny

> We walk…

Yoske

> Yeah, we saw that part.

Danny

> The children get toys, and in the evening we have a show for the children.

Yoske

> A show for the children! And what you do…

Danny

> I take a part in the show.

Gershon

> But retarded children are not…

Yoske

> The children of Ein Ro'eem aren't retarded! What's the matter with you?

Gershon

> I'm just repeating what Danny said…

Yoske

> He didn't mean it. Tell me, Danny, what is your role in the play?

Danny

> My role…

Yoske

> And what is it? What's the play about?

Danny

> I'm the bear.

Yoske

> The bear! And what's the bear doing in the play?

Danny

> Nothing…he's doing nothing.

Yoske

What do you mean, nothing? What's the play about? The show?

Danny

It's not…it's not…a serious play...

Yoske

Why isn't it serious? What's the play about?

Lea

It's a very important role that they gave him.

Yoske

Of course it's an important role! But the story…

Danny

It's not such an important role. Just…a role.

Yoske

How could the show go on without the bear?

Danny

I don't know…

Yoske

So it's a very important role!

Gershon

Do you know your lines by heart?

Danny

I don't have any lines…no.

Gershon

There aren't any lines? The bear doesn't talk?

Danny

No.

Yoske

> The bear doesn't talk! What's the matter with you? Since when does a bear talk?

Gershon

> So what's he doing?

Danny

> Jumping, growling…

Gershon

> Is that all?

Danny

> Yes.

Lea

> He loves to jump.

Yoske

> At least you don't have to learn any lines.

Danny

> Even so, it's not easy. It's really hard to walk while wearing the bear costume, and with the bear mask on you can hardly breathe.

Yoske

> You wanted to be an actor, so now you have your chance. It's not always easy. But I'm sure it's a serious role, and you'll do a good job.

Danny

> It's not serious.

Yoske

> I'm sure it is. You are very important men in the kibbutz, and if they gave you this role, it means…

Danny

> I'm not a very important man in the kibbutz…

Yoske

Yes you are!
(To Lea.)

Isn't he a very important man in the kibbutz?

Lea

Yes he is!

Yoske

Sure he is.

Gershon

Where did you meet? Have you known each other a long time?

Danny

No...no, we just met.

Gershon

What do you mean you just met?

Danny

We met not that long ago.

Gershon

If you get married, where are you going to live?

Danny

Get married...not yet...

Yoske

They aren't getting married yet! What's the matter with you? They're young. They have lots of time for all that yet.

Gershon

I say, if they're going to leave the kibbutz...

Yoske

They aren't leaving! Danny would never leave the kibbutz.

Gershon

> I say if they leave, and they haven't decided where to go, why not come to our kibbutz?

Yoske

> They know where to go. Don't worry.

Gershon

> But they don't know how is to be a member of Kfar Me'eer! For instance, our annual allowance is much bigger then in Ein Ro'eem.

Yoske

> The allowance isn't important…

Danny

> You're rich…

Gershon

> We aren't rich! We just…

Yoske

> He loves his kibbutz. That's what's important. Not the allowance.

Gershon

> No, it's just an example…it's…

Danny

> You're rich. All over the country people know. Come, Lea.
> *(Danny and Lea leave.)*

Gershon

> Not rich…but…

Yoske

> Come. Let's go. .
> *(Yoske and Gershon leave.)*

Scene 14

The small stage in the field. Irit, Amalia, and Shulamit are dressed as squirrels. Arie is dressed like a king and sitting on a throne. Mira is dressed like a magician. Alyakim and Ronny are dressed like servants.

Ronny

> Have you seen the soap in the bathhouse?

Irit

> Who's going to take a shower in the bathhouse?

Alyakim

> Even the volunteers from abroad don't go in there.

Arie

> Yes they do! They have bathrooms by their rooms, but they don't always have hot water there.

Amalia

> People who live in neighborhoods of huts in the north don't even have that much.

Shulamit

> So what kind of soap have you seen there?

Ronny

> The big, rough cubes of laundry soap!

Mira

> Every one brings his or her own soap. That's all.

Ronny

> But I saw laundry soap!

Mira

> You saw it 'cause somebody brought it there to do laundry.

Ronny

> But why can't the kibbutz provide better soap for anyone who needs it?

Alyakim

> If you bring better soap to the bathhouse, you'll see tomorrow that it's gone.

Mira

> That's true.

Amalia

> But if you forget your soap…

Ronny

> The kibbutz can give more. For instance, what kind of cigarettes do they give us? Can't they give us better cigarettes?

Alyakim

> There are worse kinds.

Ronny

> Worse than what we get? I'm not sure.

Arie

> Ronny, stop complaining. You may think…

Ronny

> Arie, you don't smoke. Do you know what Sergeant brand cigarettes are? They're like…

Irit

They call them forget-me-not cigarettes.

Mira

Why forget-me-not? Because you smoke one of those cigarettes once, and you never forget it?

Irit

No. You have to draw on it constantly, 'cause if you stop for a second, the cigarette will go out…

Alyakim

It doesn't actually contain any tobacco. It's horseshit.

Ronny

Even the cigarettes in military prison are better!

Irit

Even the…

Mira

Ronny, why don't you just quit smoking?

Shulamit

He tried, but failed.

Ronny

I didn't try.

Shulamit

As far as I remember…

Ronny

I don't know what you remember, but I didn't try.

Alyakim

You're talking about how bad Sergeant Cigarettes are, but do you really think White and Red are better?

Amalia

Whoever smokes White and Red, soon will find himself dead…

Arie

And what about Dafna cigarettes?

Alyakim

Dafna is a little bit better, but even this…

Amalia

The other day I asked a guy what kind of cigarettes he was smoking. He took the box out of his pocket and read the brand: De Pe Ne. What's De Pe Ne? He showed me the box—Dafna…De Pe Ne…It sounds like something from Paris…

Alyakim

And Sergeant Cigarettes? There are two crossed swords on the box. It's not a sergeant…it's a general…

Mira

I heard that the kibbutz gives a reward to anyone who quits smoking.

Irit

A reward? What reward?

Mira

A reward…

Amalia

A suitcase. So I heard.

Arie

Why a suitcase?

Amalia

I don't know…a reward…

Alyakim

> To pack and leave…

Ronny

> I heard that someone won the jackpot in the lottery.

Mira

> Who won?

Ronny

> I don't know…someone from the kibbutz. I heard a name…

Amalia

> What name?

Ronny

> Never mind…a name. But…

Alyakim

> Do you know or not? You…

Ronny

> I heard a name, but I don't want to talk about it.

Arie

> No one won.

Alyakim

> How do you know?

Arie

> It's all rumors.

Irit

> But how…

Arie

> I tell you. It's all just rumors.

Mira

> If someone won, and he didn't leave, he must be a very good member of the kibbutz.

Alyakim

> Doesn't it bother you that someone lives here with us and has a lot of money?

Mira

> No. As long as he doesn't spend more than other members, I don't mind.

Alyakim

> Maybe he does spend more money and you just don't know about it?

Mira

> I don't know anything about anybody. I know what I see and what I hear...and this...

Amalia

> There are many stories in this kibbutz about people. You can't even imagine what I heard...

Arie

> What stories?

Amalia

> Ah...forget it...

Arie

> Why forget it?

Amalia

> It's not really important.

Ronny

> Not important, maybe, but I bet it's interesting.

Shulamit

> She doesn't know anything. It's just...

Amalia

> So I don't know…

Ronny

> Tell us what you know, not what you don't know.

Shulamit

> Amalia…Amalia…
> *(Avner and Ronen enter with their musical instruments.)*

Arie

> Here's the band!

Irit

> Not all of them.

Alyakim

> Where are the rest?

Ronen

> They'll be here. They'll be here.

Alyakim

> When?

Ronen

> They'll be here…soon.

Arie

> What do you mean, soon?

Avner

> They caught Yudke and recruited him to help take the chickens to the new hen house. So…

Irit

> Why didn't they take you?

Avner

> Cause I escaped. I saw Arnon and Rooven Cohen going around looking for people to help, and I walked in the other direction, pretending…

Irit

> And they didn't see you?

Avner

> Perhaps they did…I don't know…

Ronny

> Lucky me—if I'd been there, they would've taken me, too.

Shulamit

> So it's you two and Yudke? That's the whole band?

Alyakim

> Band…

Avner

> Eli. The drummer.

Arie

> What about him?

Avner

> I don't know. We said…we said to meet at the entrance of the public dining room, and he didn't come…

Amalia

> What happened?

Avner

> I don't know.

Ronen

> We waited for him for ten minutes.

Avner

> And we took a chance by doing this.

Amalia

> What do you mean a chance?

Avner

> Cause Arnon and Rooven could see us…

Ronen

> Where are the other actors? Danny…

Alyakim

> The director.

Amalia

> Ro'ee.

Ronny

> And the princess. Sgula.

Ronen

> Sgula is the princess?

Irit

> Yes.

Ronen

> Why Sgula?

Irit

> Because that's what Ro'ee wants.

Ronen

> But why does he want that?

Irit

> He wants it. That's it.

Ronen

> Okay…

Avner

> So where are they?

Alyakim

> The squirrels said that Hedva took Danny somewhere.

Irit

> She came here, and at the end of the rehearsal, she took him.

Avner

> Took him where?

Amalia

> That's what we don't know.

Shulamit

> There are a lot of mysterious things going on here.

Arie

> Mysterious things…really, you may think…everyone will be on time. Don't worry.

Alyakim

> If the king says…

Mira

> Have a bit of patience, and you'll see that everyone will be here on time.

Avner

> Mira! It's you!

Mira

> Yes.

Avner

> I swear I didn't recognize you! What is your role in the show?

Mira

> I'm the magician.

Amalia

> She is the good magician.

Avner

> Good, good. It's just…you. The good magician…Good…

Mira

> If you say so...

Avner

> I think so...

Amalia

> If you think…

Ronen

> I think…earlier today we were late, and now we're early.

Amalia

> When were you late?

Ronen

> This morning. We came, we waited, Ro'ee came and told us that we were late…

Arie

> Now you're here on time, and everyone else will be on time too.

Alyakim

> And if they aren't on time?

Arie

> They will be on time.

Ronny

> We can manage without a rehearsal. It's just a show for children.

Irit

> Just…

Ronny

> What's the show about, anyway? You can tell it to the children instead of acting it out. Really. The princess takes the bear to the forest…

Shulamit

It takes her.

Ronny

So it takes her. The king gets angry. She left without saying anything to anyone beforehand. So…

Amalia

He grounds her…

Ronny

We can also show the story of King David and Uriah. I'll play King David, and Shulamit will play Bath-Sheba…

Shulamit

Really…

Ronny

No, I mean…

Irit

Ronen, are you smoking?

Ronen

No. Thank you.
(Enters Eli)

Avner

Eli! What's the matter with you? We were waiting for you!

Eli

I was working, and I…I forgot…

Alyakim

You forgot…

Eli

I forgot to look at my watch. That's all.

Ronen

> Have you seen Yudke?

Eli

> No.

Amalia

> He's helping take the chickens to the new hen house.

Eli

> The new hen house? No, I haven't seen him.

Alyakim

> And Ro'ee? Have you seen him?

Ronny

> And Sgula?

Irit

> And Danny?

Eli

> What do you want from me? I came here right after work.

Alyakim

> What kind of kibbutz is this? Everybody works! Nobody wants to play! No…really…

Mira

> We can manage without a rehearsal, and everything is going to be…all right…

Irit

> But how? We haven't even had one rehearsal with the band!

Arie

> They will play, and we will act, and everything will be okay.

Ronen

> They say that a bad rehearsal means a good show. But what happens if there is no rehearsal at all?

Alyakim

> The question is, is there going to be a show at all. I mean, according to what we've seen here…

SCENE 15

In the orchard. Jonathan, Alon, and Efrayim.

Alon

      Don't you have any grapefruits here?

Efrayim

      We do, but they aren't ripe yet.

Jonathan

      What *do* you have?

Efrayim

      I don't know…what you want?

Jonathan

      The big ones. Do you have any?

Efrayim

      What big ones?

Jonathan

      Like this. Big.

Efrayim

      I don't know…big…

Jonathan

      We used to call them *bombyles*.

Efrayim

Bombyles…

Jonathan

They're bigger than grapefruits.

Alon

Something like this.

Efrayim

Do you mean pomelo?

Jonathan

Do you have any?

Efrayim

Is that what you mean?

Jonathan

Maybe. Do you have any?

Efrayim

We do, but we can't sell them. The law forbids it. So…

Jonathan

Why is it forbidden?

Efrayim

That's the law.

Jonathan

But why?

Efrayim

I don't know. That's the law.

Jonathan

What kind of law is it?

Efrayim

>Law is law. Otherwise we would sell our fruit on the side of the road. But it's illegal to do that.

Jonathan

>Illegal?

Alon

>Come on, buy it at the supermarket.
>*(Alon and Jonathan leave.)*

Scene 16

In the field, Sgula is walking. Suddenly she hears a shout, "Sgula! Sgula!"

Sgula

> Who... ("Sgula! Sgula!")

Sgula

> Ro'ee...?
> *(Ro'ee enters.)*

Ro'ee

> Sgula! Where have you been? I've been looking for you for a long time!

Sgula

> I'm here!

Ro'ee

> I can see that.

Sgula

> And where is Danny?

Ro'ee

> I don't know.

Sgula

> Were you looking for him?

Ro'ee

Of course I was looking for him!

Sgula

And did you find him? Or Hedva?

Ro'ee

No. But I'm sure he's back by the stage.

Sgula

And what if he isn't there? Will we start looking for him again?

Ro'ee

I don't know if we'll have enough time. But...

Sgula

And then what? What if he's not there?

Ro'ee

You know what? I'll be the bear.

Sgula

You'll be the bear?

Ro'ee

Why not? I'll wear the bear costume, and...

Sgula

No, no.

Ro'ee

Why not?

Sgula

Because I want Danny to do it. That's why I insisted he be part of the show.

Ro'ee

I'm talking about in case of emergency. If Danny isn't there.

Sgula

But we have enough time to look for him. So why would we go back? If we don't find him…then we will see.

Ro'ee

I really don't know if we have enough time to look for him. The actors are sitting there waiting for us. The rehearsal…

Sgula

Ro'ee, I'm not going to do it without Danny! Let's not…

Ro'ee

So…if he's not there, you…

Sgula

I don't know…

Ro'ee

So let's go. Let's go find him.

Sgula

I'll go in that direction. You…you…

Ro'ee

Why don't we go together?

Sgula

I don't think it's such a good idea to walk together.

Ro'ee

Why not?

Sgula

'Cause if we go in different directions, we'll have twice the chance of finding him.

Ro'ee

But if one of us finds him, the other won't know, so…

Sgula

In the end we'll meet at the stage, before the show. So…

Ro'ee

You don't want to walk with me. Why?

Sgula

And why is it so important to you to go with me?

Ro'ee

You are the princess. The real princess. My princess. I love you, Sgula.

Sgula

You what?

Ro'ee

I love you. That's how I feel.

Sgula

Really?

Ro'ee

Yes. Sgula, it's not easy for me say it, but…

Sgula

Why isn't it easy? People say it all the time.

Ro'ee

Not me. I say it only when I mean it, so…

Sgula

Ro'ee, I'm glad you said it. But…

Ro'ee

You're glad?

Sgula

Yes, because I think it's good when people say how they feel. But you know we have the show this evening, so first we have to find Danny. After that…

Ro'ee

But what do you have to say about what I said just now?

Sgula

> You said…

Ro'ee

> That I love you. Yes.

Sgula

> I say it's good that you've said how you feel. It's…

Ro'ee

> Sgula, I love you. Can't you…can't you…

Sgula

> Ro'ee, we will talk about it after the show. Okay?

Ro'ee

> Will we go somewhere to talk?

Sgula

> Somewhere?

Ro'ee

> Yes! After the show! After all the work we've done together, it's good to talk…to see what we've done…together…

Sgula

> Ro'ee, we will talk about this after the show. Okay?
> *(Leaves.)*

Scene 17

In the field. Lea, three boys: Avraham, Yossi, Sasson - and a little donkey.

Lea

> Are you learning at *Mevo'ot* School? I think that I know you.

Yossi

> *Mevo'ot.* Yes.

Avraham

> Learning…hardly…

Yossi

> You don't learn…

Lea

> Do you know my brother Shlomi?

Yossi

> Shlomi Nathan?

Lea

> Yes.

Yossi

> We know him.

Sasson

> Is he your brother?

Lea

    Yes. Have you seen him around?

Yossi

    You're Lea, aren't you?

Lea

    Yes.

Yossi

    I think I saw you at school.

Lea

    Have you seen him around?

Avraham

    No, we haven't.

Sasson

    Shlomi Nathan. I know him.

Lea

    And you haven't seen him?

Avraham

    No. No.

Lea

    Where did this donkey come from?

Yossi

    We found it not far from here. It was wandering.

Avraham

    It doesn't want to go!

Sasson

    It's lazy! It hardly moves!

Lea

    It's small. What do you want from it?

Avraham

> To move!

Lea

> You push it, and it doesn't want…

Sasson

> It's lazy! That's all!

Lea

> But it belongs to someone!

Avraham

> We found it! It was wandering!

Lea

> So you took it…and…

Yossi

> It belongs to no one!

Sasson

> Now it belongs to us!

Lea

> So you can push it…

Yossi

> We have no choice! It doesn't move!

Lea

> 'Cause you…

Avraham

> We gave it a name. Vayzata.

Lea

> Vayzata?

Sasson

> That's its name in Israel! I gave it the name!

Lea

You just stole a donkey.

Yossi

We didn't steal it!

Avraham

We aren't thieves.

Sasson

Come, come, Vayzata!
(The three boys and the donkey leave. Danny enters.)

Danny

Who are those boys?

Lea

Forget it. Come.

Danny

Have they seen your father?

Lea

Come. Come
(Leave.)

SCENE 18

In the field. Amichai and six girls are sitting under a tree.

Amichai

> Girls, I have an idea. We have an hour until the car will be waiting for us at the intersection, and it doesn't take more than fifteen minutes to get there. What do you think of singing a little?

Sarah

> Singing?

Amichai

> Why not? You would be surprised by how your voices can sound in the open air. With the echo from the hills. Come on, let's stand up.

Gila

> We don't mind standing up, but singing? Is this the place? Is this the time?

Amichai

> Trust me. Singing here doesn't sound like it does in the auditorium at school. It's much better here. Get up. Malka, please take out your gum. Thank you. Let's sing "Stool at

His Feet." You girls sing it well, but there's still room for improvement.

The girls

   (Singing.)

Stool at his feet
Above him a tree
That lost all its leaves
Fall retrieves.
Waves and waves,
Waves and waves.

Amichai

Did you hear that? The echo bounces all the way from Rosh Ha'Nikra to Haifa. One more time, from the beginning. And don't push. Gently. Gently. Please. From the beginning. Racheli, you look as if you're begging the audience for forgiveness. Look more confident, please. Sing softly, but looked focused. One more time, please.

The girls

   (Singing.)

Stool at his feet
Above him a tree
That lost all its leaves
Fall retrieves.
Waves and waves,
Waves and waves.

On pomegranates he feeds,
Profusion of seeds,
Like a bell reads,
Like pearls and beads.
Waves and waves,
Waves and waves.

Apple and pear,
In the windy air,

Wishing just to share
Shelter and care.
Waves and waves,
Waves and waves.

Amichai

Not bad. Now we'll harmonize. Gila, Malka, and Sarah—start with "waves and waves." Haya, Aya Kapeliuk, and Racheli, start with "stool at his feet." Are you with me? Please.
(The girls sing.)

Very good. You may sit. We have at least ten minute before we have to go. So…you may sit. Yes.

SCENE 19

In the field. Hedva is sitting on a rock and Doobi.

Doobi

> What happened?

Hedva

> I wanted to pick several lemons, so I climbed a tree and fell down.

Doobi

> Why did you have to climb? You couldn't find any lemons close to the ground?

Hedva

> There were a few, but they were not beautiful, and I want to use them to decorate the kibbutz dining room. For Sukkot.

Doobi

> Sukkot?

Hedva

> Yeah, for Sukkot.

Doobi

> But how can you carry the lemons? You don't have a bag.

Hedva

> I don't need many. Two in one pocket, two in the other, and two in each hand

----

Doobi

> I see. And your leg. Is it broken? Sprained?

Hedva

> Sprained, I think.

Doobi

> But you're not sure? Does it hurt?

Hedva

> It's not so bad.

Doobi

> And you wanted to limp all the way back to the kibbutz...

Hedva

> Why not? Slowly, slowly.

Doobi

> I think you shouldn't walk in your condition. You could end up making your leg worse.

Hedva

> It's really not that bad...

Doobi

> If I hadn't gone to the banana plantation after stopping by the orchard, I wouldn't have met you here, and you would have walked—limped—all the way to the kibbutz.

Hedva

> I would have, yes.

Doobi

> You have to go to the dispensary.

Hedva

> Why were you visiting the orchard? Did it have something to do with the workers' strike?

Doobi

Yeah. So you've heard about the strike?

Hedva

I was by the head office this morning when you were speaking with Arnon and Zoltty.

Doobi

Ah…yes, I remember. You were there.

Hedva

You didn't want to talk to me…

Doobi

I didn't want…

Hedva

I asked you what was going on, and you didn't want to talk.

Doobi

Ah…I was…a little bit…stressed out. I'm sorry if I hurt your feelings.

Hedva

Never mind.

Doobi

Let me see your leg. Let me take a look here.
(*Looks at her leg.*)

Does it hurt when I put pressure here?

Hedva

No.

Doobi

And here?

Hedva

Ouch!

Doobi

I don't think it's broken. But I'm not a doctor. Come on. I'll help you get back. Climb up onto my back.

Hedva

Onto your back?

Doobi

Yes. I'll give you a piggyback ride. .

Hedva

Doobi, I'm not a little girl.

Doobi

I didn't say you were a little girl.

Hedva

No, but you treat me like one.

Doobi

I don't treat you like a little girl—I treat you like a wounded girl!

Hedva

I can walk, if you help me.

Doobi

Help...

Hedva

If you support me.

Doobi

Yes, but it will still hurt you to limp along by my side, and it will take a long time. Come on, get on my back.
(Hedva gets on his back.)
Okay?

Hedva

Yes.
(*Doobi starts walking.*)

Do you have the strength to hold me up like this all the way back?

Doobi

I hope so. If not, we'll make you into a ball and I'll roll you back home.

Hedva

A ball…

Doobi

Ouch!
(*Stops walking.*)

You're too heavy for me.

Hedva

But you said…

Doobi

Get down.
(*Hedva gets off his back.*)

I will support you. We'll go slowly. What's wrong? Are you okay?

Hedva

You have to support me from the other side.

Doobi

Why?

Hedva

'Cause my bad leg is on this side.

Doobi

What difference does it make?

Hedva

> It matters. My bad leg has to be the leg closest to you.

Doobi

> I don't think so. I think…

Hedva

> The injured leg must be the leg that is closest to you!

Doobi

> No. When you limp, your good leg must be close to me, and your injured leg must be on the air!

Hedva

> But I step with my injured leg on the ground when I walk! Gently, but I step on it! Even if I don't step…

Doobi

> Hedva, will you just listen to what someone else says? Just once? Believe me—I know what I'm talking about. What you say is right, but let's try, just once, something that someone else says, okay? What do you say?

Hedva

> If you insist…

Doobi

> Let's try what I suggest, and we'll see how it goes.

Hedva

> Doobi, it's my injured leg. Not yours.

Doobi

> It doesn't mean that I'm wrong. Let's try it.

Hedva

> Okay…

Doobi

> Let's go.
> *(Supports her and they leave.)*

Scene 20

In the orchard, Rudi and Nathan.

Rudi

We heard about your strike—Motke Liber and me—and we were determined to go and to talk to Zoltty about it. We told him that if the orchard workers are on strike that means something is wrong. They wouldn't sit there for nothing. We must speak with them. Maybe a special meeting of the Financial Board, but we must hear what they have say. So…

Nathan

And Zoltty agreed? A special meeting?

Rudi

Yes. Yes. After all, without him you can't summon a board meeting. He agreed to listen to you. He said he thought about what would most benefit the kibbutz when they decided what they decided.

Nathan

People in the kibbutz do whatever he says…

Rudi

Listen—you have to bring before the board things that will make people believe that you're right. That it's wrong to clear part of the orchard. Or else…

Nathan

> I think it's very nice that he agreed to summon the board.

Rudi

> Without him you can't call a meeting. Where is Kessler now?

Nathan

> I think…there…

Rudi

> What about food? Is there enough? From the kibbutz, do they bring…

Nathan

> Yes. Yes. Suzan is taking care of this. But there is…there is…

Rudi

> Suzan! Who is Suzan?

Nathan

> She's a volunteer from the States.

Rudi

> Volunteer…you like it, don't you?

Nathan

> We like what?

Rudi

> Sleeping in sleeping bags…eating from cans…

Nathan

> Like it…I don't know…

Rudi

> We, who are in the kibbutz, are working hard, while you are here having fun…

Nathan

> We work, too.

Rudi

> Come. Show me where Kessler is.
> *(Leave.)*

Scene 21

In the field. Sgula is walking. Elyakim enters.

Elyakim

    Sgula! We were looking for you!

Sgula

    Did you find Danny?

Elyakim

    No. We didn't.

Sgula

    So we have to find him! Otherwise who will play the bear?

Elyakim

    Ro'ee!

Sgula

    Ro'ee?

Elyakim

    Yes. What's wrong with him?

Sgula

    I don't know…

Elyakim

    What don't you know?

Sgula

Danny is a better bear. He knows the role.

Elyakim

But Danny isn't here! So what's wrong with Ro'ee?

Sgula

If Danny isn't here, maybe…

Elyakim

Ro'ee said that you didn't want him to play the bear. Why?

Sgula

I didn't say that I didn't want him to do it. I said that we should find Danny.

Elyakim

He came to where the stage is, totally desperate. Lost. He sat down and didn't want to talk. "What happened, Ro'ee?" No answer. We thought that maybe his mother had died. His grandmother had died. Who knows. Finally he said, "Sgula doesn't want me to play the bear." Why doesn't she want you to be the bear?" He said, "I don't know. She didn't say." So…

Sgula

I didn't say that I didn't want him to do it. I said that it's very important to find Danny. That's all. So you didn't find him?

Elyakim

No. No. Someone said that he saw him, but…but…

Sgula

Who saw him?

Elyakim

Baruch said that he saw him walking with a girl heading toward…

Sgula

A girl? What girl?

Elyakim

He didn't know. He couldn't tell. He called to Danny, but Danny kept walking. So…

Sgulva

Was he with Hedva? 'Cause she took him from the rehearsal.

Elyakim

No. Baruch knows Hedva. He would recognize her.

Sgula

So who was she?

Elyakim

I don't know.

Sgula

Not Hedva…she took him, and handed him over to someone else…

Elyakim

What? What?

Sgula

That's Hedva! She took him and gave him to some other girl, so…

Elyakim

Come on, Sgula. There is a show tonight! Ro'ee can do it. I'm telling you…

Sgula

Ro'ee thinks that it's easy to be the bear, but it's not so simple.

Elyakim

Why not? The bear doesn't talk.

Sgula

> It's not that simple.

Elyakim

> Look, I don't know what's going on between you two. You're treating him as if he did something wrong.

Sgula

> I am not. I just don't think that it's so simple to be the bear. That's all.

Elyakim

> It's just a show for children. It's not something…

Sgula

> I don't have anything against him. He can be the bear. He can…

Elyakim

> You can help him, with the role.

Sgula

> I don't have anything against him. I promise you…

Elyakim

> So come on. We don't have time. The children are waiting…

Sgula

> Okay. Okay. But I tell you, Hedva is…is…

Elyakim

> Let's go.
> *(Leave.)*

Scene 22

In the field. Danny and Moris.

Moris

> But you really have to go to Amka. There's a session with
> the rabbi, and…

Danny

> I don't like those kinds of things.

Moris

> This is about making a good match. A lot of guys have gone
> there and had good results. You have to at least give it a
> try. They say that almost everyone who goes there finds his
> match.

Danny

> I'm not going there.

Moris

> Why not give it a try? What do you have to lose?

Danny

> Listen, do you see my girlfriend? There, there, on that hill?
> She's waiting for me. I have to take her home. So…

Moris

> Your girlfriend?

Danny

> Yes.

Moris

> Where does she live?

Danny

> In …that direction. Soon it's going to be dark, and she has to get home. Her parents will be upset.

Moris

> Okay. Maybe not this time, but you should definitely go as soon as you have the opportunity. It's something…and you are not married…so…

Danny

> We don't think about marriage, yet.

Moris

> That's what I say! This rabbi is a really wonderful miracles maker. He is…

Danny

> No, no, no. Let him make wonderful miracles for other people where ever he wants. This is not for me.

Moris

> But you can…

Danny

> Did he help you? The rabbi?

Moris

> No…not me…I heard about him…

Danny

> So…you don't…you don't…

Moris

> Even if you are going home, you can…

Danny

> We aren't going to Amka. We're going to her home. That's all.

Moris

> Where does she live, anyway?

Danny

> Bait Anan. Okay?

Moris

> That direction?
> *(Points.)*

Danny

> No. That direction.
> *(Leaves).*

Scene 23

The small stage in the field in the evening. Children are sitting in chairs, looking at the stage. Arie is dressed like a king and sitting on a throne on the stage.

Arie

> Where is my daughter? Where is the princess? What has happened to her? Where has she gone? Leaving me without saying a word? Children, maybe you know where my daughter has gone? Maybe…

A child

> She went into the forest! She ran away with the bear!

Arie

> What? What? I can't hear you…

A child

> She's with the bear!

A girl

> She wants to eat lots of honey!

Arie

> She went into the forest! With the bear! Oh, dear! It's dangerous in the forest! The bear might hurt her! And I sent my servants to look for her! The bear will eat them too! I will never see my daughter again! It's all my fault! I didn't

treat her well! I told her what to do! I didn't let her eat sweet things! And now she wants honey! And my servants? Where are they? Oh! I think I hear something. Here they are!

(Elyakim and Ronny enter.)

My servants! Did you find my daughter?

Elyakim

Yes, your majesty. We found her.

Ronny

She's in the forest, with the bear.

Arie

Is she all right?

Elyakim

Yes. She is just fine, but…

Arie

Why isn't she coming home?

Ronny

She's with the bear now. She said, "I will not come home without the bear."

Arie

Without the bear…she will not…

Ronny

She said, "The bear is my friend now, and I won't come home without it."

Arie

The bear has put a spell on my daughter! It's all witchcraft! Witchcraft! Call the good magician! Call her quickly! Only she can help! What are you waiting for, servants?

(The servants leave.)

A bear in my palace! It'll wander around here and get everything all dirty! It isn't clean! It growls at night and will scare everyone! What shall we do? What shall…
(The servants enter with Mira, the good magician.)

The good magician! My servants tell me that my daughter is in the forest with the bear, and she doesn't want to come back! It has bewitched her!
(Elyakim leaves, and Ronny leaves after him.)

What shall we do?

Mira

The bear that was wandering around the palace?

Arie

Yes! It has taken my daughter! The princess! It has bewitched her!

Mira

It hasn't bewitched her.

Arie

It hasn't?

Mira

No. On the contrary. A spell has been put on the bear. He was a prince, a son of a king, but he was disrespectful. He didn't obey his father's orders. He always did whatever he wanted, and he thought only of himself. One day he did something really annoying, and his father couldn't take it anymore. The king called a witch, and the witch turned the prince into a bear. She said, "Until a girl comes along and says 'I love you,' until that happens, you will be a bear."

Arie

And can't you turn him into a prince again?

Mira

No. I do not have those powers. The only way he can be changed back into a prince is by a girl saying "I love you."
(Touches Arie's head with her magic wand and leaves.)

Arie

> If he really is a prince, I agree to allow him into the palace,
> even as a bear! He only has to behave himself. He can't eat
> the flowers. Servants! Servants! Where are they? I will fire
> them. They are never...
> *(Elyakim and Ronny enter.)*
>
> ...never...

Elyakim

> Yes, your majesty.

Arie

> Go quickly to the forest and tell them to come back to the
> palace! I agree to allow the bear into the palace, as long as
> he doesn't wander around while the servants are washing
> the floor. Find them!

Ronny

> Here they come!
> *(Ro'ee enters, dressed as a prince, and Sgula, dressed as a princess.
> The band plays.)*

Arie

> Here they are! Here is my daughter! She is all right! Thank
> God! Thank God!

Sgula

> Daddy, meet my prince! He was a bear, and the moment I
> told him "I love you," he turned into a prince! And...we are
> going to get married.

Arie

> Married? Very good...very good. Is he going to behave from
> now on?

Ro'ee

> Yes. I'll behave. From now on.

Arie

> And do you want to marry my daughter?

Ro'ee

Yes. Yes. I want to. She said that she loves me…

Arie

Good…good. I'll build you a new palace, more beautiful than my own.

Sgula

There's enough room in your palace, Daddy. We don't need a new one.

Arie

No. I'll build a new palace. Servants! Send everyone invitations for the wedding! Invitations with gold lettering and hand-painted birds. Come. Let's go. We have a lot of work to do.

(The band plays as the actors leave the small stage. The children and their nannies applaud and leave.)

(Curtain.)

OUT THERE,
IN THE FOREST

A play by Shmuel Cohavy

SCENE 1

Room in an apartment in London. Gordon and his wife Lia are in the room. Gordon is packing a suitcase.

Lia

> You can't even explain to yourself why you're going, Gordon. Not just any old evasive explanation. I mean a genuine explanation. You said it has nothing to do with your program on TV. The tours…

Gordon

> You're looking for a logical explanation…

Lia

> Your explanation is just so odd…

Gordon

> I'm not sure that I've got a logical explanation. Has everything I've done so far been logical? I'm actually trying to recall something logical…something logical… trying… trying… Where are my vests? I mean, are these all my vests?

Lia

> Logical…

Gordon

> It's just a trip, Lia! Seriously! Perhaps I'm going to see something different, something a person doesn't do every

---

day. But why is it necessary to give a logical explanation? Precisely in a case like this, precisely in a case like this—are these all my undershirts?

Lia

It's not always enough just to feel, especially not in this case when you are going to look for a criminal hiding out somewhere in a tropical jungle in Africa. You're chasing after a criminal who hides his face behind a leopard mask. Logic certainly doesn't play any part in this. Seriously, Gordon, there isn't even any guarantee that this story is true. You read something in the newspaper, and without verifying it you go off...

Gordon

Why shouldn't it be true? It was in the papers. A mysterious murderer is running wild in the East African Republic, in the bush, what they call a savanna, murdering villagers, raping women, attacking and killing white tourists. What makes you think this story is made up? What reason could there be for inventing it? Are you saying...are you saying that these are all the socks I have?

Lia

If it's true and you go to the jungle, I don't believe you'll come out of there alive. They say that he kills anyone he sees in the jungle. You look at it this way—you're walking in the jungle, at night, alone. Suddenly, from behind one of the trees, a man wearing a leopard mask lunges at you. He stops in his tracks, removes his mask, extends his hand, and says, "Mr. Gordon Blatt, I presume. Perhaps we should go to a place where there is more light so I can recount my life story to you. Are you from England? Would you like a cup of tea?"

Gordon

Lia, I'll be careful. There are things that interest me, but why does it seem obvious that I have to take risks to see them? I'm not at all certain that I'll see him, but I am certain that I'll be very cautious.

Lia

Because you have an extremely dangerous goal. That's why. You're not simply interested in looking into the man's eyes after he's arrested. You're going to look for him, and he's not particularly amiable toward people.

Gordon

The fact that I'm going does not mean that I won't take every precaution. Lots of tourists go there. People climb Mount Everest…

Lia

But they prepare for it beforehand! Do you know what kind of training they go through before they go there? And yes, not everybody makes it back.

Gordon

This belt…this belt…

Lia

You're busy with all kinds of things, Gordon. Trying all kinds of things. Once you were a serious tourist and now you're busy being interviewed and telling jokes that have nothing to do with real tourism.

Gordon

They love that on TV…

Lia

You keep trying different things and I have to act as a cushion, absorbing your tears. By your own admission it didn't work too well this time, but now you have a new plan that is more interesting by far, and I'm supposed to sit here, doing my best to understand, explain to friends, answer telephone calls from all over the world, and to top it all, try to comfort and encourage you, to show empathy…and now suddenly TV no longer interests you, and it seems, in fact, that they have lost some interest in you too—that's what you said...

(The telephone rings. Lia goes to answer it.)

Gordon

If it's the TV guys, I'm not home...

Lia

Why? You want to get rid of them, don't you? Then tell them...

(Lifts the receiver.)

Gordon

I don't...I'm not...

Lia

(Speaking into the receiver.)

Yes. Yes. Elizabeth! Yes, right. I've been there. You're absolutely right. No, she isn't. I completely forgot about it. Elizabeth, I'll call you tomorrow evening and we'll discuss it then, okay? See you.

(Replaces the receiver.)

Elizabeth.

Gordon

Lia, I have to look the man in the eye. To catch a glimpse at least, to see what's there. Once at least.

Lia

To see what?

Gordon

I don't know. I truly have no idea. Should I take a tie? An umbrella?

Lia

A tie! Really! In the jungle! As if you were going to Oxford Street in London. Do you have to make a fool of yourself? Is that your way of protecting yourself? As soon as you get the chance to become something serious like a real journalist, you start making fun of the entire situation. But this time you are also risking your life and I'm supposed to sit here and worry. Sit here waiting for the telephone to ring. It may be a call from you. Perhaps it will be someone else, like a reporter who needs some explanations. Maybe it will be a call from your concerned parents or from our embassy in the East African Republic—what are you looking for? I think you've finished packing.

Gordon

I haven't finished. Not yet. Lia, there are a few other things…things that have to be…I don't want to open my suitcase at the hotel and see—By the way, I also intend to buy a handgun when I get there.

Lia

Do you think a gun will help you in the forest, at night?

Gordon

He doesn't commit his crimes in the forest…so…

Lia

The gun? It doesn't shoot in the forest?

Gordon

No! The man in the leopard mask. I think I heard them say that…

Lia

And if you look into his eyes, do you think all your problems will be solved and just disappear? Your drinking problem, for instance? What about our relationship with all its ups and downs?

Gordon

I didn't claim that my problems would disappear. I simply want to do something worthwhile, something that's not just fleetingly frivolous, and you're angry, you're completely against it. Why?

Lia

Gordon, I have no intention of sitting here waiting for the telephone to ring.

Gordon

Come on then, come with me. I want you to come with me. *(Takes her hand.)*

Imagine we're in a jungle, at night. Duck your head. Duck your head. The branches are low. Be careful. It's swampy here. What did you step on?

Lia

The floor.

Gordon

Watch out, there are snakes here. Can you see that over there? It's a lion. It's sleeping.

Lia

You're serious…you're actually being serious. I see.

Gordon

I'm extremely serious! But shhh…are you interested in seeing the jungle by night?

Lia

Just one look into the eyes of the man with the leopard mask, and you turn serious.

Gordon

I find it simply fascinating. What's he hiding? What's behind the mask?

Lia

And you really believe that one look into the eyes of this murderer will turn you into a serious person?

Gordon

> I won't become serious, because I already am serious, Lia.

Lia

> The critics say that your performance on your program about tourism issues provides all the entertainment—it's full of jokes, jibes. They say that your so-called research is pathetic, but you don't understand...

Gordon

> I'm finished with TV, Lia. Finished with them.

Lia

> Did you inform them that you quit?

Gordon

> I'm not going to appear on any more of their tourism programs. All the jokes and jibes are over, finished!

Lia

> Have you told them?

Gordon

> No, but that's not important. What is important is—

Lia

> You're about to go away and you haven't told them?

Gordon

> When I return from Africa...

Lia

> On the other hand, you yourself said that there have been indications, following the reviews, that they may try to get rid of you.

Gordon

> True, but despite the reviews, O'Hara said that he was behind me, that he backs me up.

Lia

And the boss?

Gordon

The boss too, the boss too…

Lia

They'll fire you eventually. But you'll be interviewed on the rival channel! Impressions of a journey to Africa. A glimpse into the eyes of the leopard man!

Gordon

This is a private matter, this trip to Africa! I don't want to tell anyone about it! Why won't you believe me? I'm not so important that anyone would want to ask me about it! I want to prove to myself—

Lia

What are you going to do when you get there? Where will you go?

Gordon

There are probably guided tours into the jungle region, the bush. I'll look into it and see. Perhaps I'll get help from the staff at the British Embassy. I'm sure there are people in the hotel who could help.

Lia

Help how? By pointing you in the right direction? To where the dangerous murderer is hiding? Do they give advice about how to gaze into his eyes?

Gordon

I'll find out where he operates, in which region, in the same manner that anyone would ask for general information. I won't tell them that I want to actually get near him—or maybe I will, depending on whom I ask. Then we'll see. But I will definitely be careful. I want to return home.

Lia

There'll be a surprise waiting for you when you get back.

Gordon

You'll be here, Lia. You'll be here to listen to all my stories, to receive my gifts…

Lia

Primitive art…wooden sculptures…

Gordon

You'll be here, Lia.

Lia

I'm not sure about that. I'm just not sure.

Gordon

You won't be sorry if you wait for me. This time you won't regret it.

Lia

Our partnership no longer exists.

Gordon

I know that I'm a bit strange sometimes, but I'm always thinking about how you'll react, what you'll say. I love you. I want you to be here.

Lia

And I love you, but I'm not sure I'll be here. I'm not going to wait until the end of your escapade, if you return at all, just to face yet another one in its wake.

Gordon

You'll be here.

Lia

I'm not sure. I can't guarantee it. And be careful not to come back with some disease…not that I care that much.

Gordon

What disease?

Lia

You know damn well what disease is rampant in those parts.

Gordon

You're treating me like a small child who can't look after himself.

Lia

I don't know how to relate to these things, but I don't have the energy.

Gordon

Would you like me to call the airport
(Glances at his watch)

and cancel my flight? Seriously?

Lia

The truth is, I don't really care what you do anymore.

Gordon

The flight's in three and a half hours. They won't refund my money.

Lia

That's what's important to you. I understand.

Gordon

Do you really think I'd endanger myself? That I'd wander around the jungle alone? Without protection? In prohibited areas?

Lia

Do whatever you like, Gordon. I won't be sitting here biting my nails, waiting for news from you. I won't be here waiting for you with a hot meal and a warm bosom, with an attentive ear for all your adventures. I will also not be here to identify

the remains of your body. I simply won't be here. Gordon, you've done all sorts of things, jumped from one thing to another, but this is the first time you've done something that endangers your life. Not really. I feel as if I have to look after you, run after you—
(The telephone rings. Lia picks up the receiver and speaks into it.)

Yes. What? Yes, one moment.
(Lia hands the receiver over to Gordon and speaks to him.)

It's the TV guys. The manager.

Gordon

I'm not here. I've already left.
(Closes his suitcases and starts for the door.)

Lia

Tell him yourself. Don't run away.

Gordon

Tell him I'm in a hurry. I'm out of here. See you. Have I got my wallet? Yes. It's in my pocket. See you.
(Leaves.)

Lia

(Into the receiver.)

He's in a big hurry. He already left. This minute, he left just this minute. This very moment. He'll call you. What? I don't know. Perhaps. He'll call you. That's what he said. Hello? Hello? Hello?
(Lia hangs up the receiver.)

SCENE 2

Hotel room in Abilda, the capital of the East African Republic. Present in the room is Akilla, a high-ranking Foreign Ministry official, and Dabbon, a minor Foreign Ministry official.

Akilla

> The English are pretty naive. Behind their famous English manners lies a lot of naivety. They believe anything they are told. We can exploit this not only for the good of the Republic, but also to benefit the revolution.

Dabbon

> The revolution?

Akilla

> Yes, the revolution.

Dabbon

> How can an Englishman, however famous an explorer he may be, be of any help? The revolution is an internal issue.

Akilla

> I've already told you—first of all he can help with the rampant public health issues here. The fact that someone like him, who is so well-known in England, can visit during a time like this…

Dabbon

> If I understand it correctly, it's a personal visit.

Akilla

We've got to make use of what we can, personal or not. We can use it for our purposes by publicizing his visit as well as his account of what he sees here. Then, when we take control of the government…

Dabbon

Then he'll tell everyone how pleasant we are, based on his experience meeting us during his visit to the East African Republic?

Akilla

We're going to need international support and recognition.

Dabbon

And he will help us with this…

Akilla

He'll tell them back home that the people who took part in the revolution were very hospitable toward him and took good care of him. We can't ignore these things, Dabbon. That's our job. It's good PR for the Republic as well as for the revolution. I summoned you here because there are several things I want you to do later concerning this issue and I didn't think it would be appropriate to discuss these things in the hotel lobby. That's why we came up here.

Dabbon

I hope there are no microphones here.

Akilla

So do I. We've already said enough this evening for us to face a firing quad tomorrow. But aside from the revolution, I regard this Englishman as your project. He'll travel extensively around the country, he'll see animals, travel by Land Rover between the lakes and through the nature reserves. It will be your job to remind him that there are people here too, not just animals. There is poverty and disease here that we can overcome with the help from wealthy nations.

Dabbon

And he'll convince the wealthy nations?

Akilla

He'll play his part, at least in convincing British citizens. Keep in mind their feelings of guilt. We've got to give it to them slowly, in small doses. It doesn't sound so nice, but that's our job.

Dabbon

On one hand you claim that his coming here shows there's nothing to be afraid of in the East African Republic. On the other hand, you want him to see all the poverty and sickness...

Akilla

First let him enjoy himself. That's the initial step. Make him feel good here. We'll show him all the beautiful thing this country has to offer. Then, gradually, we'll start showing him other things—but only after he feels good here, when he has formed a positive emotional attachment to this place...

Dabbon

I'm sure he's coming here to enjoy himself...

Akilla

We won't stop him from having a good time. We'll simply make him aware of our problems and appeal to his conscience. Dabbon, if you want to rise to an important position such as mine in the Foreign Ministry someday...

Dabbon

I'll do it, Akilla. I'll do it and you can rely on me. I'm just not sure that this is what we should do right before the revolution begins. Are we sufficiently prepared for such a move? I'm not sure. Our president—

Akilla

There's still time before the revolution. The problem is…

Dabbon

I'm not convinced that we're ready. We keep putting it off, but instead of doing something useful…

Akilla

You don't know all the facts, Dabbon. There are some things I can't tell you, and there are some things I myself do not know.

Dabbon

Now we're busy with this Englishman…

Akilla

Because it's part of our work! We mustn't stop working, and we don't know when the revolution will happen, so we can't…

Dabbon

You're relying on the generals—

Akilla

On the colonel.

Dabbon

On the colonels—

Akilla

Colonel!

Dabbon

Colonel. You're relying on him, but he's only looking out for himself. We are sitting…

Akilla

The truth is, Dabbon, we can't do it without him.

Dabbon

> He and his soldiers are going to stage the revolution. And then what? Where are we headed? What do we believe in? Nobody talks about these issues.

Akilla

> The first step is to get rid of the current president. That's the most important thing. To end this tyranny. That in itself is not a minor feat.

Dabbon

> And then what?

Akilla

> We're working on it, Dabbon, believe me.

Dabbon

> Will we go back to being a true democracy?

Akilla

> Eventually, absolutely.

Dabbon

> What do you mean by "eventually"? When?

Akilla

> I don't have a simple answer, Dabbon. I don't think that at this stage we are ready for it. These things take time.

Dabbon

> Is there going to be a kind of council that will decide these things?

Akilla

> We will have all these things. We'll discuss this too when the time comes.

Dabbon

> We'll discuss…

Akilla

> Can you pull off the revolution without that officer, Bono Kali? I won't prevent you, Dabbon. Stage a revolution. Do you think I'm happy about every single thing? We can't accomplish everything at once. I also know that prior to overthrowing the king and taking control of the government, Benzazi pledged that he would improve the state of the nation. He didn't exactly manage to do this. But this time the colonel is not alone. We are a considerable group.

Dabbon

> There was a group then too.

Akilla

> That was a group of officers. We are a group of citizens. Don't forget that today we have a more influential press, and he's going to need legitimization. Without us, he won't get the support he needs. I also think that he really cares. I have spoken to him on numerous occasions. I'm not denying that there are some risks, but in the meantime I suggest that you concentrate on your work in the Foreign Ministry. It's important. I'm talking about the Englishman.

Dabbon

> I'm under the impression that you don't trust me, Akilla.

Akilla

> I'm relying on you, Dabbon, and I'm sure you're going to do a good job.

Dabbon

> I was referring to the revolution.

Akilla

> I do trust you, and I want to give you a very important mission. In fact that's what I wanted to talk to you about. I definitely want you to play host to the Englishman, but I also have a special mission for you for tomorrow.

Dabbon

On the way here you hinted at something far from the capital. Something not so…

Akilla

It's something important, Dabbon, everything is important. It seems to me that you disregard details that seem unimportant to you. Let me remind you that I earned my senior position in the Foreign Ministry after years of fulfilling minor positions, some of which I have told you about. That's just part of it. You want to run the entire world, but you forget that…

Dabbon

I don't want to run anything and I don't ignore detail. I just think that not enough discussion is taking place about what we want to achieve with this revolution. That's all.

Akilla

I'm sure you'll play your part when the time comes.
(The telephone rings. Akilla picks up the receiver.)

Hello. Yes. Vaccination? Who? No, he hasn't arrived yet. Should be arriving soon. Yes. Yes.
(Hangs up the receiver.)

Vaccinations…

Dabbon

What did you want me to do?

Akilla

About what?

Dabbon

You said before that you wanted to give me a special mission.

Akilla

Yes. The Horai Tribe—they are loyal to the president. He comes from there. They are near the border of the Raizer

Reserve. I heard that the Tourist and Development Ministry official in charge of the reserves is abroad. This is my plan: we'll open the reserve and remove some herbivorous animals, claiming that the reserve is overpopulated and there isn't enough food to go around. This will please the villagers, as they are allowed to hunt animals outside the reserves. But when you free the herbivores, the carnivores follow. If you allow a herd of deer to roam outside the reserve, it's impossible to prevent a lion who wants to stalk the deer from exiting. They're extremely nimble. We'll of course warn the villagers that predatory animals are wandering around in the region. We'll let a few lions and leopards loose. This will make the villagers very wary and they'll think twice about organizing demonstrations in favor of the president.

Dabbon

They'll hunt the lions and the leopards.

Akilla

So be it. Anyway, they'll be occupied with issues other than helping him or perhaps warning him if they notice any of the preparations for the revolution. Look, this may not prevent them from doing things, but this is primarily a diversionary tactic. They'll be busy hunting and watching their backs. It will certainly make it more difficult for them to get organized.

Dabbon

What would they be capable of doing anyway? They are so far from the capital!

Akilla

You never know. One mustn't overlook even the smallest detail when planning a revolution, Dabbon. One detail, another detail…

Dabbon

Do you have the authority to do this?

Akilla

> You will have the authority to do this. We'll provide you with false papers, the colonel will provide some soldiers to accompany you…

Dabbon

> Me?

Akilla

> Yes, you. Why not? From tomorrow morning. You'll go to the—

Dabbon

> What about our visitor from London?

Akilla

> You'll speak to him, make arrangements with him—anyway, you're not going to spend twenty-four hours a day together. You must—

Dabbon

> But why tomorrow? You say that you don' t know when the revolution—

Akilla

> You do your job…
> *(The door to the room opens and Gordon walks in, followed by a bellboy carrying his suitcase.)*
> Mr. Gordon Blatt?

Gordon

> Yes.

Akilla

> We are from the Foreign Ministry of the East African Republic. I'm Akilla. This is Mr. Dabbon.

Dabbon

> *(Shaking Gordon's hand)*
> How do you do?

Gordon

How do you do? Foreign Ministry? They mentioned something at the reception. What's the matter?

Akilla

First I'd like to apologize…
(The bellboy puts down the suitcase and turns to leave. Gordon hurries after him and gives him a tip. The bellboy leaves.)

I'd really like to apologize profusely for invading your room. It was important for us to meet you immediately upon your arrival in our country and we were afraid we would not notice you in the lobby. We obtained permission to wait for you in your room. So first of all, please accept our apologies.

Gordon

Okay. Okay. But what happened? There must have been some kind of mistake. The Foreign Ministry?

Akilla

You're a renowned person in England, and we thought…

Gordon

Renowned person?

Akilla

The hotel informed us that you were expected, and you are very well-known in England.

Gordon

Well-known?

Akilla

That's what we were told. An explorer. Is this not so?

Gordon

I am well-known, but as a TV personality, not so much as an explorer.

Dabbon

But you are well-known?

Gordon

Yes, that's right. How can I help the Foreign Ministry?

Akilla

On the contrary—we want to help you. Lately, due to our president's capriciousness and the spread of disease, we have earned a bad name in the West. We would like to show you that things are not so bad in this place. We want to show you things— of course we don't want to interfere with your plans to see what you want to see. Therefore…

Gordon

But I'm not representing anyone, so I don't know…

Akilla

You don't owe anyone anything. We know that you are not representing anyone. You…

Dabbon

It's common practice for famous people, even if they are here in no official capacity, to receive a special welcome. It does not obligate you at all. What are you interested in seeing?

Gordon

I want to see what everyone else comes to see. The jungle, animals, things like that.

Dabbon

We'll help you. We'll also show you things others don't see. Whom did you want to contact? Have you contacted any specific agency?

Gordon

I haven't contacted anyone. I had intended to ask someone at the reception tomorrow whom to contact. Perhaps even our embassy.

Akilla

> He
> *(Points at Dabbon.)*
>
> will give you his telephone number, and you will call him within two to three days.

Dabbon

> If you need anything, call
> *(Takes out a business card and hands it to Gordon.)*
>
> We'll help you in any way we can. Try to coordinate your plans. Some things can be dangerous for someone who isn't familiar with this place.

Gordon

> I heard there is a man who hides behind a leopard mask and kills people left, right, and center.

Akilla

> That is so.

Gordon

> Where does he hang out, this man?

Akilla

> Why do you ask?

Gordon

> So that I'll know where to be careful.

Akilla

> If you go where all the tourists go, or anywhere with Mr. Dabbon, you have nothing to fear.

Dabbon

> Nevertheless, I'm interested to know. Where does the killer roam around?

Akilla

> Mr. Blatt, I'm sure you have deranged murderers in England too.

Gordon

Nonetheless, where is he? In the city? In the country?

Akilla

In various places. Not in the capital, so there's no need for you to be concerned. And I promise you, Mr. Blatt, he will soon be caught.

Dabbon

Lately he has been active in the southwestern part of the country.

Gordon

Are those tourist areas? Are there any animals there?

Akilla

There are several reserves there that tourists visit.

Gordon

Which reserves?

Akilla

There are all kinds...

Dabbon

The Ape Reserve, the Raizer Reserve, as well as several others.

Gordon

The Raizer Reserve?

Akilla

Raizer. Yes.

Gordon

Has he been seen in the reserve?

Akilla

Near the reserve.

Dabbon

> He murdered a little girl there. She had wandered out of her village and was found later. Her body.

Gordon

> How do they know that he killed her? Couldn't it have been someone else?

Akilla

> He was seen running away.

Gordon

> He was seen?

Akilla

> Yes.

Gordon

> Does he leave any special signs? How does he kill?

Dabbon

> Usually with a knife. Sometimes he strangles his victims.

Gordon

> It could be quite interesting to see this man. Not that I intend…

Dabbon

> Let's hope you don't see him.

Gordon

> Why not?

Dabbon

> Because if you do, it will be the last thing you see. So pray that you will not see him.

Gordon

> Why does he commit murders? Does anyone know anything about it?

Akilla

No one knows.

Gordon

Hasn't he said anything?

Akilla

Not that we know.

Gordon

Interesting…murderer I can understand. But why the leopard mask?

Dabbon

We'll know once he's arrested.

Akilla

And this will be very soon, I promise.

Gordon

But isn't anyone interested? Isn't everyone wondering what he actually wants?

Akilla

He's a crazy murderer. What's there to know? Deranged.

Gordon

Perhaps he's not insane.

Akilla

Maybe. There are murderers and crazies everywhere. Would he be wearing a leopard mask if he were sane?

Gordon

I don't know…

Dabbon

When the English ruled in Kenya, guerilla warriors who fought against them used to wear leopard skins, so perhaps…

Gordon

But he's killing locals, isn't he?

Akilla

He has also murdered whites. But when a person is insane…

Dabbon

Perhaps he wants to terrify people. Seeing a leopard's face suddenly appear before you is very frightening.

Akilla

Well, Mr. Blatt, I'm sure that you didn't come all this way just to see this murderer. And if you do want to see him, you can do so after he's captured. We will leave you now. Do you have Mr. Dabbon's card?

Gordon

Yes.

Akilla

Call him. Not tomorrow, as he will not be available. He'll be back in a couple of days.

Dabbon

You won't be sorry. You'll see things that a regular tourist doesn't get to see. Au revoir!

Gordon

Bye.
(Akilla and Dabbon leave. Gordon starts unpacking his suitcase. The telephone rings. Gordon picks up the receiver.)

Yes. Yes. What? Vaccinations? Oh, okay. I'll see tomorrow… what? Okay. Tomorrow.
(Hangs up the receiver.)

SCENE 3

Cave on the edge of the jungle in the East African Republic. Susan and Betty are inside. Betty is slicing meat. Susan is trying to light a fire by rubbing two stones together beside a pile of dry leaves. She gives up and tosses the stones aside.

Susan

> There's got to be another way to light the fire.

Betty

> Haven't I ever explained the rope method to you?

Susan

> Rope?

Betty

> You take some rope, hold it in both hands, hold it next to a log and start…
> *(Demonstrates.)*
>
> …rubbing it from side to side.

Susan

> I don't see any log around here, do you?

Betty

> Then let's go out and look for some.

Susan

> What about rope?

Betty

> Rope is made by weaving thin branches together.

Susan

> It isn't so easy, this weaving together. After the fire is lit the rope will burn and we'll have to make some more.

Betty

> There's no shortage of thin branches, Susan—you're just too lazy to go outside, that's all. Besides, if we look after the fire, we won't have to keep rekindling it.

Susan

> Then our cave will fill with soot.
> *(Picks up the stones and tries again, unsuccessfully.)*
>
> Just one spark will do it…

Betty

> You're ruining your fingers by doing it that way!

Susan

> Wait a minute, I think—

Betty

> Not like that! You're just being stubborn, Susan. It doesn't work that way. Are you trying to prove something? I don't understand. And you're supposed to be the practical one.

Susan

> I agree that this isn't the best method, but we'll have to find a solution so that we won't have to keep going outside to gather thin branches to make more and more rope that's just going to burn up. True, stones do break, but…

Betty

> So do your fingers! Susan! What are you trying to prove to yourself?

Susan

(*Tosses the stones aside.*)

I have absolutely no ide—in fact, what are we trying to prove by sitting here in this soot-blackened cave? When is Rachelle supposed to come back?

Betty

She should be here any second now. Why?

Susan

Perhaps she'll bring a few branches.

Betty

We wanted to live in the jungle, in Africa. It's not so easy. If you're getting upset about a fire, I don't know, perhaps we've failed.

Susan

Wouldn't it have been simpler just to bring some matches?

Betty

We wanted to prove that we could survive anywhere, under any circumstances. Even in a cave near an African jungle. Without husbands, without children, without running water, and even without matches. We've haven't done too badly over the last two months or more…

Susan

Two months?

Betty

Yes, at least. More likely three months.

Susan

Have you retained a sense of time?

Betty

Absolutely. It's one of the things one has to learn.

Susan

What day is it today?

Betty

Well, I don't know for sure.

Susan

How long do we have to be here in order to prove to ourselves that we can survive under any conditions?

Betty

We can't determine a specific time, Susan. But listen, nobody's keeping you here against your will.

Susan

I think we've already proved that we can manage fine.

Betty

Doesn't seem to me that you're managing— not with the fire.

Susan

My hands hurt. I've already lit several fires by rubbing these stones together.

Betty

Stop insisting on using the stones. There are other ways that are supposed to be easier and quicker.

Susan

It's worked before. But seriously, Betty, how are we going to know that we can manage, that we're prepared, that we are capable of coping with any eventuality?

Betty

Are you waiting for a sign, a signal, something that will clearly indicate that we have established our independence? A deadline? Something clear and explicit that says, "It's over".

Susan

Yes, I do expect something—I don't mean something official, but definitely a clear sign. How else will we know?

Betty

We'll know. You can be sure of that. Besides, aren't you enjoying this? True, there are some difficult moments, but not everyone gets here, and we'll never have another opportunity to live in a place like this. Not many people experience what we're experiencing here. Aren't there any beautiful moments, Susan? Moments to remember? Isn't this strengthening our friendship?

Susan

It's already strong...

Betty

We should go home only when we feel we've done it all, felt it all, and experienced everything, so that they'll envy us at home. And most important of all, so that we won't feel that we've run away and returned home because we were uncomfortable, because we didn't have the energy to continue. That would be disastrous for us, Susan. The way we'll feel when we get home is more important than how they'll see us.

Susan

I don't feel that I have to prove anything to anyone.

Betty

To yourself, Susan, primarily to yourself!

Susan

I've already proved it to myself, I think.

Betty

Have you proved it all to yourself?

Susan

All? I don't know. There's always more...

Betty

Don't you have any enjoyable moments?

Susan

Sometimes. Yes. Don't you miss home sometimes, Betty?

Betty

I don't think about it, Susan. We're going to go back home at some point, but in the meantime…

Susan

Don't you miss your husband, your kids?

Betty

Susan, we're here, and I promise you we won't be here forever. Can you bring some water? I'll take care of the fire.

Susan

We're running away from something, Betty. We're running away. Vacations are meant to last a month, two months, but we've been here for almost three months, according to you. I've already lost all sense of time.

Betty

I'm not running away from anything and I'm convinced that you'll eventually thank me for everything we're experiencing here.

Susan

I do thank you, and it's…

Betty

Every day here seems different, holds something new. Each day we grow by learning to cope with a new problem. There's no routine. We have learned how to cut meat, *(Waves her knife.)*

how to hunt meat, how to kindle a fire. How to maintain personal hygiene despite difficult conditions.

Susan

True, we learned how to bathe in a stream.

Betty

Do you want to bring some water? We won't be able to cook without water.

Susan

What are we eating today?

Betty

That.
(Points to the meat).

Rats. Good enough for you?

Susan

Seriously, Betty, couldn't we have found somewhere else in the world to spend our time? Two weeks here would have been great, but there are also other places, aren't there? There are other places in Africa, Asia, even in Europe. But the bottom line is that I don't have a sense of great adventure here, of an important struggle. What I'm experiencing is simply a series of all kinds of problems—what part of the rat is edible, which shit from which animal makes the best fuel…

Betty

Do you want to eat or not? Get some water. Do me a favor.

Susan

The smallest village in Mexico is more interesting than what's happening here. That's the truth and you know it, Betty. There aren't even any animals around here. They're all in the reserve. Does anyone even know that we're here? Is anyone looking for us?

Betty

Why should anyone be looking for us? We told them we'd be travelling in Africa for at least two to three months and that we'd send a postcard every now and then. So what's the problem? Besides—

Susan

> I promised my husband to call once a week.

Betty

> And have you considered that perhaps your husband and kids are just a little happy to have gotten rid of you?

Susan

> I don't know…

Betty

> You can be sure they are.

Susan

> My husband can hardly manage without me. He doesn't have a clue how to make an omelet.

Betty

> So he'll learn. You do everything for him at home, and it suits you both. While you're here, he'll learn. He won't have any other option.

Susan

> He won't learn a thing. The house will be a mess, filthy, dishes everywhere, and I'll have to clean it all up. It's not as if he doesn't try. He cares a lot, but always…

Betty

> My husband can't do anything but open a can of beer, like they do in the movies! Like this, *splishh!* But other than that…

Susan

> No, my husband really tries…

Betty

> Don't you ever feel like a maid at home?

Susan

> Sometimes, but when I get back—

Betty

> You give in to them. You mustn't.

Susan

> Don't you ever give in?

Betty

> No. Not easily.

Susan

> So is the atmosphere at your home always tense?

Betty

> Not really. But I don't yield easily. I don't give in to myself either. It's very easy to say, "Why argue? Just let it go." They, however, take advantage of this. We mustn't give in.

Susan

> Betty, why do I always get the feeling that you know everything, manage beautifully, handle whatever…

Betty

> I certainly don't cope in all situations, and when we get back we'll find that our problems haven't dissipated. But I enjoy being here and I think that both sides, us and our families, will benefit from this time apart.

Susan

> But why? In spite of everything…

Betty

> Are you going to get the water?

Susan

> Okay, but first one more question. Give me the answer when I get back. Why did they invent the faucet? Matches? The refrigerator? So that we can learn to live without them?

Betty

Why do people travel? Why do people climb mountains? Why do they feel pleasure when remembering what they've experienced?
(Rachelle enters the cave, holding a bundle.)

Rachelle

(Waving the bundle in her hand.)

I've brought some rabbits and rats that are larger than the traps.

Betty

We're not short of meat. We're short of water. Didn't you go past the stream?

Rachelle

I did, actually, but I didn't have the jar with me.
(Peeks into the jar standing in a corner of the cave.)

There's enough, I think.

Susan

I'm going out.
(Starts to exit the cave.)

Betty

What about the water?

Susan

Rachelle says there's enough.

Rachelle

It won't do any harm to bring some more.

Susan

There's enough.
(Leaves.)

Rachelle

What's up with her? She's very irritable.

Betty

> She's had enough of being here.

Rachelle

> Had enough?

Betty

> Just when it's starting to get fun.

Rachelle

> Fun?

Betty

> Sure! Aren't you having a good time?

Rachelle

> Are you?

Betty

> Why not? I'm not saying there aren't any problems, but it always feels great when we overcome them.

Rachelle

> Didn't we come here to suffer?

Betty

> To suffer? What are you talking about? We came to cope with problems, not to suffer.

Rachelle

> Perhaps Susan is suffering.

Betty

> It's not easy for her, but when we get back in a month or two, she'll be proud of what we did here.

Rachelle

> A month or two?

Betty

> The good times are only starting now, Rachelle! By the time we got used to things and got organized…

Rachelle

> Two months?

Betty

> What's the matter, Rachelle? Are you suffering too?

Rachelle

> I'm not suffering! I'm missing home. Don't you, sometimes?

Betty

> Yes, sometimes. But this is also something we should learn to overcome, Rachelle. It's part of our quest. Put the meat here.

Rachelle

> First we're supposed to overcome our yearnings, and then we get to go home?

Betty

> Then we know that we can return home with equanimity.

Rachelle

> By that stage we won't want to go home.

Betty

> Why not?

Rachelle

> Because we'll no longer be missing home.

Betty

> We will. But that shouldn't be a reason to run back home. We'll control the situation, not be controlled by it. That's all. Have you thought about that, Sister Rachelle?

Rachelle

> No, I haven't thought about it, Sister Betty.

Betty

> We have to feel that we're ready, Rachelle. I don't know about you, but I don't feel ready yet, not quite.

Rachelle

> I don't know whether I'm ready or not. I just know that I'm missing home.

Betty

> We haven't learned how to cope in any situation yet. There are so many things we don't know how to do. We haven't even detached ourselves yet. I mean, we still care about what everyone at home is going to say, and how they'll manage without us. I think we've got to cut ourselves off. What they'll say doesn't matter! Let them say what they want! Cut off! Detach! Do you understand?

Rachelle

> Detach from what? How is it possible to just detach?

Betty

> To feel independent. So that nobody can tell you what to do. So that you're doing the things you're doing not simply because your husband, children, neighbors, or the entire world expect you to.

Rachelle

> Why should I care about doing what's expected of me, if I feel good doing it?

Betty

> Don't you want to be strong and independent?

Rachelle

> And being here is what will make us strong and independent?

Betty

> Absolutely.

Rachelle

> Mostly we're learning how to pee outside with a torch in one hand and how to—

Betty

You're missing the point, Rachelle, and that's that we're managing in extremely harsh conditions, which is something not everyone would be able to do.

Rachelle

If they weren't given any other option, many people would survive in these conditions, I guarantee you. But, Betty, if you're enjoying this, it gives me pleasure to see you flourishing here. That's fine.

Betty

(*Peeking into the water jar.*)

There's still a bit of water. Perhaps it's enough. Put the meat you brought here, in the pantry. We'll eat it tomorrow.

Rachelle

(*Moves the meat.*)

I think I'll bring some water anyway.

Betty

Listen, Rachelle, haven't we learned to overcome our fears here, including the fear of going outside in the dark with a burning torch in order to pee?

Rachelle

Overcome the fear? I didn't have this fear at home. That's because I simply didn't have to go out in the dark with a torch to pee there.

Betty

So now you know that you had this fear and have succeeded in overcoming it.

Rachelle

So I've overcome it. So what?

Betty

The point is, you've defeated it.

Rachelle

> What option did I have? Did you want me to pee here in the cave?

Betty

> Don't you remember how frightened you were at the beginning, and I had to go with you? But eventually you did it. We also proved to ourselves that we can cope with more difficult tasks. Going out in the middle of the night with a torch and moving three hundred, four hundred yards away from the cave. Don't you feel proud of yourself for this achievement?

Rachelle

> Of course I feel proud. But I don't know how I'd feel if I encountered someone on the way. Maybe I'd faint.

Betty

> What could you possible come up against? There are no animals around here.

Rachelle

> What if the man with the leopard mask suddenly appeared out of nowhere, his strange eyes radiating terror? Wouldn't you pass out?

Betty

> I'd threaten him with the burning torch, and he'd retreat.

Rachelle

> He'd knock the torch out of your hand before you even knew what was happening to you and then you'd see his glinting knife in front of your eyes.

Betty

> I'm not afraid of him.

Rachelle

> You should be afraid of him. Tarzan won't be there to rescue you at the last minute.

Betty

> Tarzan?

Rachelle

> You said we'd be like the Three Furies, like in that movie, with black pigmy servants at our beck and call, and they'd make sacrifices to us and bow low whenever we pass them in the cave, and Tarzan would come…

Betty

> The three Amazons from that old movie…well, I wasn't that serious when I said all those things.

Rachelle

> In your heart of hearts you still yearn for him to come and be totally overwhelmed by us, don't you?

Betty

> Tarzan? If he existed at all and if he came, I assume he'd be impressed by what we're doing here. Our being here, living here, is a very compelling feat. I have no doubt about it.

Rachelle

> But Tarzan isn't going to come. Who have you demonstrated this strength for?

Betty

> The show of strength is for ourselves, for our own sense of wellbeing, to prove something to ourselves, not to anyone else.

Rachelle

> Do you by any chance have any political ambitions, Betty? No, it's okay. It's absolutely legitimate.

Betty

> I don't have any political ambitions because I don't want to tell anyone else what to do. But back home in the States, do you have the opportunity to be so independent? To

struggle with these kinds of things? At home, everyone expects you to be beautiful and shut up. Your husband may respect you, but does he genuinely honor you? All of us women must eventually return to our lives, go back to being housewives and caring for the kids. Or accompany our husbands to all sorts of important functions. I want us to return filled with self-confidence and to feel that we've accomplished something that others have not. You know, Rachelle, I recently read a *National Geographic* article about a team of women that climbed Mount Everest. I'm sure that when they returned home they—

Rachelle

Those who returned home. As far as I remember, some of the girls didn't make it. I also read the article.

Betty

There are risks, certainly. I'm not saying there aren't. It's part of the whole—

Rachelle

Don't you miss your husband sometimes? Don't the kids need you?

Betty

I miss them all, same as you and Susan. And we'll go back— just not yet. We'll eventually go home, even if Tarzan comes begging. Even if he arrives at the last minute, we won't look back. We'll simply go. That's it.

Rachelle

He's not going to run after us.

Betty

No problem.

Rachelle

Now you're putting him down all of a sudden.

Betty

No, I'm not. He's only human…

Rachelle

Isn't he immortal?

Betty

If he comes here, it's a sign that he's human, with the same fate as the rest of us.

Rachelle

Have I ever told you how he died and was resurrected?

Betty

Who?

Rachelle

Tarzan.

Betty

In which movie?

Rachelle

Not in a movie. In a book. *Tarzan and the Bedouins*, I think.

Betty

Tarzan and the Bedouins? Is there such a book?

Rachelle

Yes, there is.

Betty

What is he doing with the Bedouins?

Rachelle

They come to him. They're wandering near the jungle. They wander around a lot and reach Africa. Anyway, someone tries to murder him in the book.

Betty

Who? The Bedouins?

Rachelle

No. They host him in their tent, treat him very hospitably. But there was an evil guy there who wanted to murder the Bedouin chief, and for some reason, he also wanted to kill Tarzan. He was very cunning. At the same time a stranger was visiting the Bedouin tent. He was in a terrible condition and pretty disoriented as a result of his experiences in the jungle. An American, I think. The evil Bedouin succeed in convincing the confused American that Tarzan, who was also being hosted by the Bedouin, wanted to kill him.

Betty

Kill whom?

Rachelle

Kill the confused American, who himself is a pretty cruel guy and whose black servants, who had been carrying his equipment, had abandoned him in the middle of the jungle. He is almost savaged by a lion and saved himself by climbing up a tree at the last minute. He reached the Bedouin tent in an exhausted and confused state at the same time that Tarzan is there. Then the evil man, who wanted to get rid of the Bedouin chief, convinces him that Tarzan wanted to kill him.

Betty

Why would Tarzan want to kill him?

Rachelle

I don't remember all the details. Perhaps the evil Bedouin convinced the American that in the tent where Tarzan was sleeping, there was someone else whom the American had a genuine reason to fear. Anyway, he was persuaded to go to this tent, to stab him in the heart and flee. And the American did it. He creeps into the tent and…and…

Betty

Stabbed Tarzan?

Rachelle

> Yes. Stabbed him and fled. In the morning they came to his tent and because they knew he was sleeping there, they didn't open the blood-soaked blanket he was wrapped in. They just took him like that and buried him in the jungle he loved so much.

Betty

> Just like that? They buried him?

Rachelle

> Yes. That's what it says in the book. But it turns out that Tarzan had been forewarned, he had eavesdropped…

Betty

> But why did the evil man want to kill Tarzan? I understand that he wanted to kill the Bedouin chief, but why Tarzan?

Rachelle

> I don't remember anymore. Maybe Tarzan would have prevented him from killing the kind leader of the tribe. In any event, after the evil man and the murderer part ways— the conversation between the evil man and the confused, frightened American had transpired in the dark, among the Bedouin tents—so after the American, clutching the knife in his hand, left, the evil man felt fingers clutching at his throat. It was Tarzan. "If you scream, Tolog," said Tarzan, "I will kill you on the spot."

Betty

> Tolog.

Rachelle

> Yes, that was his name, as far as I can recall.

Betty

> Tolog.

Rachelle

> Yes. Tarzan then held him, stuffed his mouth with a rag or something, tied him up, wrapped him in a blanket, and put him in his bed. Then the confused American came...

Betty

> In whose bed?

Rachelle

> In Tarzan's bed. In the tent Tarzan was supposed to have been sleeping in. The man convinced by Tolog that Tarzan wanted to kill him killed Tolog. He thought that he had killed Tarzan. The next morning they took him, without opening the blanket, and buried him.

Betty

> In the jungle?

Rachelle

> Yes.

Betty

> Don't they look before they bury—
> *(Dabbon enters with two armed soldiers and a local villager.)*

Rachelle

> Someone's coming, and it's not Tarzan.

Betty

> Who are you?

Dabbon

> Hello, I am Dabbon from the Foreign Ministry. I was told that there were a few white women in the cave. I see that this is so. Are you living here alone, like this?

Betty

> Yes. Why?

Dabbon

> How are you managing here? Is there water around here?

Rachelle

>   There's a stream not far away, over there.

Dabbon

>   And food? What are you eating?

Betty

>   Whatever we find. A variety of things.

Dabbon

>   Do you hunt? Cook?

Betty

>   We hunt. Why?

Dabbon

>   I'm sorry, but you have to vacate this cave by tomorrow morning.

Betty

>   Why?

Dabbon

>   We are about to release animals into this area.

Betty

>   But we're not in the reserve. Why animals?

Dabbon

>   There are too many animals in the reserve.

Betty

>   What do you mean "too many"? Isn't there enough space for them?

Dabbon

>   There's enough space, but there's no food. I mean there is, but not enough to feed all the animals.

Betty

>   Not enough greenery? Leaves?

Dabbon

There are too many animals. The balance has been disturbed.

Betty

You're opening the gates? Just like that?

Dabbon

Not exactly. We don't allow all the animals to leave, but quite a large number of animals will wander out of the reserve. Yes.

Betty

So why do we have to vacate? Are we bothering anyone?

Dabbon

You're not bothering anyone, but you are at risk. Predators may also wander out of the reserve now and then.

Betty

We can handle it.

Dabbon

No, you can't. And I won't allow you to endanger yourselves.

Betty

There are villagers around here. Won't they be affected?

Dabbon

They've also been warned and they won't leave their villages until all the carnivores have been rounded up. But you here…

Rachelle

What does this have to do with the Foreign Ministry? You mentioned that you were from the Foreign Ministry.

Dabbon

There's no connection. I am simply standing in for someone. That's all.

Betty

> By tomorrow morning…

Rachelle

> But there are animals here. I saw…

Dabbon

> There are no animals around here.

Rachelle

> I saw…

Dabbon

> Ma'am, there are no animals around. Perhaps you saw some kind of small animal that escaped from the reserve, but as a rule there are no animals here. Maybe a pet belonging to one of the villagers. Besides that…

Betty

> Look, sir, we are not small children. We can look after ourselves.

Dabbon

> Ma'am…

Betty

> We'll hole ourselves up in the cave. We have water here, and fire…

Dabbon

> Ma'am, there's nothing to discuss. This is not open for discussion. I don't need the newspapers writing about two women being savaged after the animals are released into the area. Are you Americans?

Rachelle

> Yes.

Dabbon

> Americans…

Betty

> Do you have anything against Americans? If we were from Finland, would that make a difference?

Dabbon

> I have nothing against Americans. I just don't like it when they come here and think they can do what they like and tell everyone else what to do. That's what I don't like.

Betty

> We aren't telling anyone what to do. Did you hear us telling anyone what to do?

Dabbon

> Ma'am, I told you. This is not open for discussion.

Betty

> Sir, we've been here a long time. We aren't…we aren't…

Dabbon

> Ma'am, there's nothing to discuss and I'm not interested in having soldiers drag you out of here. So save me that.

Betty

> We'll sign a statement that you aren't responsible for our safety.

Rachelle

> We're not little kids.

Betty

> We've been here for over two months. We've never…

Dabbon

> I don't care how long you've been here. Tomorrow morning you are out of here. The bus to Abilda stops not too far from here. And it would be inadvisable to have the soldiers drag you out of here. And I am mentioning this out of respect for you, American or not.

Betty

> To Abilda?

Dabbon

> Yes, our capital. The bus stop isn't far from here. Ask around and the locals will tell you where. Goodbye.
> *(Turns to leave the cave.)*

Betty

> Mr. Dumbon…

Dabbon

> Dabbon, Dabbon.

Betty

> Mr. Dabbon, do you have any idea what we have been through here in this cave? What we have coped with since we've been here?

Dabbon

> No, I have no idea. I can only imagine.

Betty

> We've experienced many difficult situations. We can handle this problem too. And believe me…

Dabbon

> Ma'am, I've told you that there will be no argument! This is not the United States of America! This is the East African Republic! That's it!
> *(Leaves with the soldiers.)*

Betty

> How they can do such a…a…

Rachelle

> They're chasing us out.
> *(Dabbon enters the cave.)*

Dabbon

> Tomorrow morning. Don't forget.

Betty

> Okay! Okay!
> (*Dabbon leaves.*)
>
> They're kicking us out because of some animals!

Rachelle

> It looks like there no other option, I'm afraid.

Betty

> Why no other option?

Rachelle

> Do you want to deal with leopards and lions?

Betty

> I'm not sure it's quite legal. Warning has to be given at least six months in advance.

Rachelle

> Why? Did you buy this place? Does it belong to you?

Betty

> I didn't buy it, but I have a foothold. We have a hold on this place.

Rachelle

> Appeal to the supreme court of the East African Republic.

Betty

> They just want to frighten us. To get us out of here. They aren't going to bring animals here.

Rachelle

> Do you want to be dragged out by soldiers? You can't fight them.

Betty

> They're testing us. And we have to withstand the test. Rachelle, this is our most significant moment. We mustn't panic.

Rachelle

> But what are you going to do? Fight the army?

Betty

> We're entitled to demand an alternative place.

Rachelle

> Where?

Betty

> Wherever. As long as they provide us with a place.

Rachelle

> And if they don't?

Betty

> We mustn't give in. This place is ours. We have learned to live here, to manage. We've cleaned it…

Rachelle

> You didn't buy it.

Betty

> I don't want us to feel banished, humiliated.

Rachelle

> Banished from the Garden of Eden. Betty. There's nothing you can do against the army.

Betty

> We can at least argue, demand an alternative.

Rachelle

> They're not kicking us out because we're women, or because we're foreigners. They're genuinely bringing animals here and don't want to endanger us.

Betty

And what about the local villagers? Are they chasing them out too?

Rachelle

Not chasing out, just warning them. He said so.

Betty

But they are chasing us out, chasing us…

Rachelle

I'm going. I'm not staying.
(Turns to leave.)

I think Susan will go too.
(Leaves.)

SCENE 4

Bar in the capital of the East African Republic. Gordon is sitting with Ramsey, an American. There are several locals in the bar. The bartender is serving drinks.

Gordon

    They tell me you've seen him.

Ramsey

    Kino…another one…

Gordon

    That's what they say.

Ramsey

    Kino…another one.
    (The bartender serves them and returns to his place behind the bar.)

    Here, drink up.

Gordon

    I've had enough.

Ramsey

    That's enough? I thought you Brits…

Gordon

    No, it's just that I personally have a problem with—

Ramsey

Drink a little, but don't cut it out altogether!

Gordon

I've had some, I've had some.

Ramsey

Is that what you call drinking?

Gordon

You've seen him.

Ramsey

Who told you?

Gordon

I've been told. It's not relevant who.

Ramsey

At your hotel?

Gordon

Not important. Someone mentioned it.

Ramsey

Do they give out this kind of information at the hotel reception?

Gordon

Drop it. I have my sources. Have you seen him or not?

Ramsey

I saw him, but only for a few fleeting seconds.

Gordon

He entered your tent.

Ramsey

Who told you? That's true. We set up camp for the night not far from the jungle, in a savanna. We lit a small fire in the camp to keep out predators. I woke up in the middle of the night and heard a rustling noise, footsteps. Someone was stepping on stones, twigs. The flaps of the tent opened and I saw the little fire outside. Someone stepped into the tent. I thought it was one of us. I lit a candle and saw a leopard in front of me. A leopard standing and looking at me! On two legs. With long claws and gleaming eyes. Everything. He approached me. I drew my gun from under the pillow and aimed at him. He stopped in his tracks. He said "Get out of here!" in English, turned around, and fled. I saw his shadow on the tent for a second or two, and he disappeared.

Gordon

Why didn't you shoot him?

Ramsey

I don't know. He wasn't carrying any weapons, and it wasn't clear what he wanted. But mainly because I didn't think it was really the man in the leopard mask. Why would the leopard man choose my tent? I was sure it wasn't him. But perhaps it was not specifically to me…who knows?

Gordon

Was he carrying a knife?

Ramsey

Not that I could see.

Gordon

Is he white? You couldn't see, I know, but could you tell from his speech?

Ramsey

I don't think he's white.

Gordon

Why not?

Ramsey

I don't know. Why should he be white?

Gordon

>I don't know, I just…maybe…

Ramsey

>Drink something, drink…

Gordon

>I can't drink a lot.
>*(Gordon drinks.)*
>
>I want to overcome my drinking problem.

Ramsey

>Here? You've chosen to overcome your drinking problem in this place?

Gordon

>I didn't choose this place, but tell me, how do you know he's black?

Ramsey

>I just assume so. Would a white man come here—

Gordon

>What accent did he have?

Ramsey

>Difficult to tell, honestly. Do you think he's white? Why?

Gordon

>I'm interested to know who he is, and why he's doing what he's doing. That's it. I just thought he might be white.

Ramsey

>It's not impossible, but I find it hard to believe. I don't remember his accent. One doesn't pay attention to accents under those circumstances.

Gordon

>So you don't think he's white.

Ramsey

No, I don't think he's white.

Gordon

Did his demand to get out of here seem like a personal issue, or a more general, political one?

Ramsey

What do you mean by political?

Gordon

Perhaps he wants you out of the Republic because you're white.

Ramsey

I have no idea. Look, he's killed many blacks, so…

Gordon

But he didn't kill you. He told you to get out.

Ramsey

I don't know what he would have done if I hadn't pulled a gun on him.

Gordon

Do you think he might have killed you if you hadn't challenged him with a gun?

Ramsey

How could I know?

Gordon

Didn't you see a knife in his hands?

Ramsey

You've asked and I said no, but there's no telling what would have happened if I hadn't woken up. He's already killed people by crushing their heads with a rock or by strangling them, so there's no way of knowing.

Gordon

It seems to me he just wants to be left in peace.

Ramsey

We didn't seek him out. On the contrary, he came to us, entered our tent.

Gordon

Perhaps you invaded his territory.

Ramsey

His territory?
(Takes a drink.)

Since when is it his territory?

Gordon

He may have considered it so. That it's his territory. And you invaded it.

Ramsey

His territory?

Gordon

Were there any animals in that area?

Ramsey

No, not predators, anyway.

Gordon

Maybe he regarded it as his area.

Ramsey

So he kills anyone who enters without notice?

Gordon

And are you sure he wanted to kill you?

Ramsey

Do you think he entered my tent, late at night, wearing a mask, just to tell me to get out of there? Don't forget, he halted the moment he saw my gun. Not before that.

Gordon

Perhaps he…
(*A local man stands up and starts shouting, raises his fist, then goes back to drinking*).

What does he want?

Ramsey

He's drunk…irritable.

Gordon

Is it something political? Something against us?

Ramsey

No…just drunk. And like all drunks, he's angry at the entire universe.

Gordon

Why did he raise his fist?

Ramsey

That's their symbol, the symbol of opposition to the president. They don't like him. I can understand them. He's no small murderer, this president. Although I can't complain— he has helped me quite a bit.

Gordon

With what?

Ramsey

Helped me…helped me…to meet people here…high officials.

Gordon

You claim he's a murderer.

Ramsey

Like many African rulers.

Gordon

And he helped you?

Ramsey

> He helped me. Yes. Because of him I can move around here freely, enter areas that not everyone has access to. I obtained licenses to represent foreign commercial organizations. Listen, some very important countries, including yours, have economic ties with him, so that...well, overall I have gained by it.

Gordon

> One's got to make a living somehow, is what you're saying.

Ramsey

> Your country sells arms to him! And do you think your government doesn't know what he's up to?

Gordon

> Doesn't he ask anything of you in exchange?

Ramsey

> Nothing. His country profits from my business here. I profit too, but so do they. He talks to me here and there, tries to get some information from me about what's going on in the field. What I see and hear from people I meet. Not that he needs me as a source, but all the same...

Gordon

> He wants to check your loyalty to him.

Ramsey

> I've never told him anything significant, anything he doesn't already know.

Gordon

> What's your line of business?

Ramsey

> I try to promote projects. There are people out there in the world who are interested in what's happening here, and there are...

Gordon

What were you actually doing in the savanna at the time when this guy entered your tent?

Ramsey

Just on a trip, a safari.

Gordon

You told me before we came in here that some people know who he is, the leopard man, and where he comes from. That he in fact escaped from an institution for the mentally ill.

Ramsey

This is one of the theories, and there are testimonies to back it up. There was a case several months ago of a mental patient escaping from a local institution. Obviously there's no proof that he's the murderer, but some have decided that he is. By the way, the hospital reported that the patient was also suffering from a terminal illness.

Gordon

Cancer?

Ramsey

Could be. Or perhaps something else. There are all sorts of diseases here.

Gordon

So he's dying.

Ramsey

If it's true, then yes.

Gordon

Is he black, this sick man?

Ramsey

Of course.
(*The local man stands up again, yelling and screaming, waving a fist. He walks around and returns to his seat.*)

Gordon

> It's scary.

Ramsey

> Nothing to get nervous about. Drink, drink.

Gordon

> Nothing to get nervous about…
> (*Drinks.*)

Ramsey

> Don't be nervous.

Gordon

> You're used to it.

Ramsey

> Doesn't anyone in London ever get drunk and start yelling?

Gordon

> It happens, and it's not pleasant there either. But there I'm on my home turf. Tell me, if he's suffering from a terminal disease, perhaps he's already dead, the man in the leopard mask.

Ramsey

> Anything's possible, Mr. Gordon.

Gordon

> So he escaped, and started murdering…

Ramsey

> Somebody said that a friend of the guy that escaped, his roommate, told him that he wanted to kill someone before he died. A newspaper reporter wrote about this, but there's no knowing if this is true. According to the reporter, the friend told him that the escapee wanted to encounter the ultimate experience. That's what he said.

Gordon

> The ultimate experience.

Ramsey

That's what he said. Even if it's true, and the reporter wasn't making it up, don't forget that this guy, his roommate, is also a mental patient. So it's difficult to know.

Gordon

Couldn't it be that the escapee did in fact say this to his roommate? Why should he lie?

Ramsey

Not exactly lie, but perhaps he fantasized. A reporter arrives, asks questions, so you invent an interesting story. Who's going to listen to you if you don't have anything interesting to say?

Gordon

But perhaps he didn't invent it.

Ramsey

Perhaps. Have some more to drink.

Gordon

The ultimate experience... Perhaps he thinks that by murdering someone else, he can extend his own life, which is running out.

Ramsey

Anything's possible, Mr. Gordon.

Gordon

And why the leopard-skin mask?

Ramsey

I have no idea.

Gordon

It seems to me that he doesn't just kill people. He sentences them to death. Just as a judge dons a judicial robe, he first dons the mask, then kills.

Ramsey

It's difficult to understand how the mind of a man like this works. It seems to me that you're overanalyzing it in an attempt to find some sort of deeper meaning in all of this.

Gordon

But a leopard costume is very significant, don't you think? It means something.

Ramsey

Means what? Do you think this costume is his main issue?

Gordon

No. I presume that murdering is the main issue. But murderers don't usually dress this way, so I'm interested in knowing what statement he wants to make.

Ramsey

It sounds like you're saying that murder isn't the main issue, but rather what the murderer's trying to say by committing—

Gordon

No, I'm simply interested in knowing why he does it, and I think his costume is a significant part of the answer to this question.

Ramsey

And you're not prepared to accept that he's just some insane guy who doesn't want—

Gordon

And he does it in the forest. He operates in that area.

Ramsey

Maybe that's why he dresses like a leopard, to blend into his surroundings.

Gordon

But why does he go there? I can understand why he would want to blend into the surroundings, but why choose that specific region?

Ramsey

Maybe that's the place he can express his murderous impulses by saying to his surroundings, "I'm dangerous! I'm a murderer! I'm a leopard! I'm warning you! I can't do this in town, but here, among the bushes, I can. Here it's legitimate. I'm a leopard among leopards!" Besides, he can hide there.

Gordon

But out there in the savanna wild animals could kill him, couldn't they?

Ramsey

From my understanding, there aren't too many wild animals where he operates.
(Gestures toward a woman across the bar.)

You see that lady? Her...that one...she's a high-class call girl. She won't go with just anyone. Look, they're leaving now. Over there. He's also not just anyone, the guy she's leaving with.

Gordon

Do you know him?

Ramsey

No, but it's obvious he's a somebody.

Gordon

She's beautiful!

Ramsey

Sure is, and she has style too.

Gordon

Do you know a lot of people here?

Ramsey

Here…I've been here for five years already.
(The local man gets up yet again and yells something, waving his fist. Two other locals join in, waving fists and singing).

Gordon

What are they singing?

Ramsey

It's a song, a well-known song that goes, "I want to be free like a fish in the sea, then I'd be able to swim to wherever I want. I want to be free like a bird in the sky, then I'd be able to fly to wherever I want. I want to be free like an elephant in a field, where everyone respects him and nobody stops him."

Gordon

Do you understand the local language?

Ramsey

Not too well, but it's a popular song.

Gordon

Is it a political song?

Ramsey

No, it's a folk song. But without a doubt these men mean politics.
(The locals finish singing the song and wander around chanting rhythmically. Two policemen enter with batons and start beating the three singers. The men fall to the ground and try to exit the bar to escape the blows. They manage to leave, and the policemen chase after them).

Gordon

Why the beatings? Does the regime consider such demonstrations dangerous?

Ramsey

> I don't know if they're dangerous, but the police seem to think so. I don't think the president has anything to fear from guys like that. But you never know. Perhaps the local police commander is taking the initiative to make an impression on someone, probably a superior.

Gordon

> Those were some serious blows...

Ramsey

> This isn't England, Mr. Gordon.

Gordon

> Nor is it America, but you seem to feel at home here. *(Drinks.)*

Ramsey

> Because I've been here for a long time, and there's also plenty of beauty to be found here as well.

Gordon

> For example?

Ramsey

> You'll see for yourself soon enough. You haven't seen anything yet.

Gordon

> I want to go out and find this beauty. I can sit and drink in a pub like this back home.

Ramsey

> There are all kinds of things here too. Shows. Too bad you weren't here two weeks ago. I don't mean here in this bar, but at a nightclub not too far from here. A local singer performed holding a leopard mask in front of her face. That's how she sang, with this mask in front of her, the mouth cut open so she could sing. At one point while

she was singing she removed the leopard mask and wore a cat mask instead. Suddenly she was no longer this leopard, but a cute little kitten. At first it wasn't very pleasant to see someone in a leopard mask, especially for someone who has seen the real thing. But then I calmed down…

Gordon

I want to see the real thing. That's why I am here, Mr…. Mr….

Ramsey

Ramsey.

Gordon

Mr. Ramsey. I would very much like to see the real thing.

Ramsey

And do you think you'll be able to survive here as I have? Kino! Kino!
(The bartender approaches. Ramsey points to the glasses. The bartender pours.)
Drink.

Gordon

I've had enough. Really. So do you know where I could find him?

Ramsey

I don't have a clue. He has been seen near the Ivory Reserve, in the Bazatu Lake region, near the Raizer Reserve, not until now. That's where he was last spotted. But I don't know if you should—

Gordon

The Raizer Reserve?

Ramsey

Yes.

Gordon

Where did you see him? Where was it?

Ramsey

It was in a totally different area. On the other side of the country.

Gordon

How can one get there?

Ramsey

Where?

Gordon

Where he was last seen.

Ramsey

By bus, or by private car…you're not drinking.

Gordon

Perhaps I'll rent a car…it's possible to do so here, I presume.

Ramsey

But how are you going to manage there? What will you do? Will you sleep in a sleeping bag by a campfire? It's not the Wild West, Mr. Gordon. Do you really want to wander around between the villages, between the reserves, hoping to meet the man in the leopard mask?

Gordon

I'm determined to it - at least try.
(Drinks.)

Ramsey

Listen…
(A local man enters the bar, approaches Ramsey and Gordon, and opens his coat, to reveal a display of watches dangling from the lining of his coat.)

Gordon

What does he want?

Ramsey

> He wants to sell you a watch.

Gordon

> Thanks. I'm not interested. I already have a watch. I don't need another one.
> *(The local man closes his coat and leaves.)*

Ramsey

> Listen, I can take you there in my car, leave you there not too far from one of the tribes, but I want to make sure we have the same story in case we're stopped and questioned. We should say that we were suddenly separated and you were wandering around looking for me. Because…whatever happens to you…

Gordon

> Are you afraid they'll blame you? Isn't anyone allowed to wander around that area alone?

Ramsey

> It's not illegal, but it's dangerous. And if something happens, they'll question me, and that can be very unpleasant. It's true I plan to leave here soon, very soon, but…

Gordon

> Are you returning to America?

Ramsey

> Yes. I've had enough here.

Gordon

> Did you make enough money?
> *(Drinks.)*

Ramsey

> Yes, and the ground is starting to shake under my feet. I don't know how much longer this president will last, and due to the fact that I have had considerable dealings with him…

Gordon

   Do you think he's about to be overthrown?

Ramsey

   I don't know…he's strong, but here it's impossible to tell.
   I've been here for long enough.
   (Drinks.)

Gordon

   Do you have any specific information about an imminent
   revolution?

Ramsey

   Drop it. Forget about it. Actually, I'm going to meet him
   tomorrow evening.

Gordon

   What for?

Ramsey

   Just to thank him…for everything.

Gordon

   You're going to meet the president…well…

Ramsey

   Yes, but it's not—

Gordon

   So can you take me there, the area where the leopard man
   was last seen?

Ramsey

   Yes. In the morning. It will cost you, of course. It's not a
   short trip. Do you have a camera?

Gordon

   No, why?

Ramsey

   You need a camera, so they'll believe you're a tourist.

Gordon

> And if I don't have one?

Ramsey

> Buy one. Tomorrow morning. Without one, who knows what they'll think you're doing there. Buy one. Do you agree to stick to our story? That we became separated and you're looking for me?

Gordon

> Yes. No problem. Do the villagers there speak English?

Ramsey

> Usually it's possible to find someone in every tribe who can speak English. Tell them you're lost. They'll take you in. Take money with you as well.

Gordon

> I'll manage. I'll manage.
> *(Drinks.)*

Ramsey

> But don't wander around outside the village at night. Have you been vaccinated?

Gordon

> Yes.

Ramsey

> Don't even think of screwing without a condom. Vaccinations don't protect you from all diseases. You might also need a weapon. You'll be wandering around alone…

Gordon

> A pistol?

Ramsey

> Yes. Do you have one?

Gordon

> No.

Ramsey

> I'll try to find something for you, but I can't promise anything. It also depends on you not saying a word to anyone about who gave it to you.

Gordon

> That's obvious.

Ramsey

> Anyway, I hope you won't find yourself in any life-threatening situations. I feel responsible.

Gordon

> I won't be careless. I'm a very responsible man.

Ramsey

> I'll try to get a weapon for you. Just make sure you never have to use it.

Gordon

> I'll be careful, I'll be careful. But since there are dangers, perhaps it really is necessary. The murderer was deterred by your gun, after all.

Ramsey

> I woke up in time. If I hadn't woken up...who knows.

Gordon

> Would he have killed you?

Ramsey

> I assume he would have.

Gordon

> I'll manage.

Ramsey

> Don't tempt fate.

Gordon

> I'm not like that. I'm careful.

Ramsey

> Do you plan to write an article about it? A sort of "I met the leopard man face to face" thing?

Gordon

> It's not that, believe me.

Ramsey

> If you think about it, what are the chances that you'll even see him?

Gordon

> Mr. Ramsey, I know that the chances of seeing the man with the leopard mask up close and personal are slim to none. Believe me, I'm aware of this. But at least I will have tried. I have no intention of telling anyone about it or writing about it. I'll simply tell everyone that I went on a trip to Africa. But at least I'll be able to say that I tried to do something special, something out of the ordinary. So will you take me there? Tomorrow?

Ramsey

> Yes, but first I'll take you back to the hotel. Are you alright? You sound...

Gordon

> I drank a bit too much. It'll pass.

Ramsey

> You are a bit...drunk.

Gordon

> It'll pass...
> *(Shouts.)*
> It'll pass! It'll pass!

Ramsey

> All right, come on now. I'll take you back to the hotel.
> *(Leaves some coins on the table and helps Gordon stand up.)*
> Come on, I'll take you home.

Gordon

It'll pass…

Ramsey

Come on, come on.

Gordon

I'm…I'm…it's just…it's just…

Ramsey

Come on, it's okay. We'll be there soon.
(Ramsey supports Gordon as they leave the bar.)

SCENE 5

Betty and Rachelle are in a hotel. Rachelle is packing. Betty is walking around in a robe, drying her hair with a towel.

Rachelle

> We did what we could, Betty.

Betty

> I'm not so sure.

Rachelle

> One can always do more.

Betty

> Let's just admit it, Rachelle. We failed. We ran away.

Rachelle

> We did not! We had to leave.

Betty

> Imagine Susan returning to the cave and not finding us. We left without even leaving a note.

Rachelle

> We had no other option, Betty. We told the soldiers that she hadn't come back yet. I'm sure they looked for her and brought her straight back here, to Abilda. She may even be on a plane back to the States by now.

Betty

> On a plane? Do you really believe that?

Rachelle

> It's possible…

Betty

> They've already found her, she's already in the capital, and now she's already on a plane? By the way, I'm not sure she would agree to get on a flight without knowing what happened to us.

Rachelle

> Maybe she knows.

Betty

> How would she know?

Rachelle

> They might have told her. The soldiers could have told her.

Betty

> She wouldn't get on a plane without talking to us. Maybe we shouldn't agree to fly home either. She wouldn't leave without talking to us, without knowing for sure what has happened to us.

Rachelle

> Susan is always very practical, very pragmatic. If she knows that we're alive and well…

Betty

> Practical…

Rachelle

> She's always been like that.

Betty

> She's the one who suggested we go to the nearest town to buy some matches! Is that what we came to Africa for? To buy matches at the grocery store in the nearest town?

Rachelle

> That's what made her practical. I think I've packed everything…

Betty

> She doesn't know how to light a fire!

Rachelle

> The soldiers must have found her after she went down the wrong path and had to sleep in a tree. They must have brought her here, to the capital. She probably went to the embassy, got money and papers, got on a plane…

Betty

> She wouldn't leave without talking to us.

Rachelle

> The soldiers probably told her we're fine, and that was probably good enough for her.

Betty

> She wouldn't fly without talking to us.

Rachelle

> I'm sure they've found her. There are villagers there—there are people there.

Betty

> We should never have left the cave without her.

Rachelle

> We had no other option! Even you were scared of those soldiers.

Betty

> It's exactly what I said before. We ran away. We got scared.

Rachelle

> Should we have fought the soldiers?

Betty

> We could have resisted…

Rachelle

> Resisted how?

Betty

> We could've done something. But tell me, if Susan is so practical, why didn't she come back to the cave last night?

Rachelle

> It's impossible to tell what might have happened to her. Maybe she went for a walk, got lost, and didn't make it back to the cave by nightfall.

Betty

> You don't know but you're not worried.

Rachelle

> I didn't say I wasn't worried. But it's also possible that everything's fine. Come and sit down. Have something to drink.

Betty

> I'm sure she wouldn't have left without us.

Rachelle

> What choice did we have? They said they were bringing in some animals and there might be several predators included. So what could we…

Betty

> I hope Susan didn't run into one of those wild animals.

Rachelle

> By the time they bring in the animals, which might include a predator or two, the villagers will have found Susan and provided her with protection. They don't open the gates for the animals to stampede out. It takes time. Do you want some Coke? Whisky?

Betty

Predators…

Rachelle

She won't come across any wild animals. Worst case scenario, she'll meet that little fawn that I saw.

Betty

That adorable little Bambi that followed you?

Rachelle

Right! You remember!

Betty

You couldn't understand what it was doing wandering around on its own.

Rachelle

I still don't understand.

Betty

They opened the gate to the reserve for a few seconds to let someone in or out, and it leaped out. That's all. They closed the gate and it was trapped outside, its mother still inside.

Rachelle

Your hair is dry, Betty. Come and have something to drink.

Betty

So it saw its mother on the other side of the fence. It was outside and she was inside.

Rachelle

It followed me but kept its distance. When I stopped, it stopped too, looking at me like this…waiting…

Betty

It needed a mother, but I don't know…

Rachelle

> Why did it stop whenever I stopped?

Betty

> Probably because you didn't really look like its mother.
> *(Sits down.)*
>
> It was testing you. Is this my mom? Is this not my mom? My kids, for example…

Rachelle

> Kids? They're sixteen, seventeen already.

Betty

> That's what I'm saying. They're not kids anymore, but they still haven't learned…
> *(Knock on the door. Rachelle opens it. A hotel employee enters carrying a bucket.)*

Employee

> I…to clean…

Rachelle

> Okay, okay.
> *(The employee takes the bucket to the bathroom.)*
>
> Betty, I'm just as concerned as you are about Susan. But we have to realize that the fact is we took an enormous risk when we decided to embark on this adventure.

Betty

> Is that what we're going to tell Susan's family?

Rachelle

> I don't know what we're going to tell her family, but we have to admit to ourselves that we took a risk.

Betty

> A risk, yes. But we should have done something last night. When it started getting late, we should have taken torches and gone out to look for her.

Rachelle

> We fell asleep. We woke up this morning to find the soldiers standing at the entrance to the cave.

Betty

> We fell asleep because we thought everything was fine, that she'd come back, but she didn't, and we still have to speak to her family.

Rachelle

> Back to reality, Betty! Speaking to her family is part of the real world!

Betty

> We were in the real world. A different one, one that we don't experience every day, but…

Rachelle

> I don't know. Sometimes I think that Susan was right when she told you that this entire adventure is an escape for you. Things aren't easy for you at home, Betty, with your husband and kids. Not that it's always so easy for me either.

Betty

> It wasn't an escape. It was to experience something else. That's all it was.
> *(The employee exits the bathroom and starts to make the beds.)*

Rachelle

> But you said that your husband and kids…

Betty

> I like to talk, so I talked about them. Don't you have problems at home?

Rachelle

> Betty, if you need any help at home, we are willing…

Betty

> Help? We came here to learn how to cope with extraordinary things, and you're offering to help me at home?

Rachelle

> Perhaps your true challenge lies at home.

Betty

> I'm not running away from any challenges.

Rachelle

> At home you don't face the dangers you face here, and perhaps it's hard for you without risks.

Betty

> It's not the risk. What risk? It's only now that they're bringing in these predators. There weren't any before.

Rachelle

> The man with the leopard mask.

Betty

> What about him?

Rachelle

> Isn't he dangerous? I hope Susan didn't run into him.

Betty

> So do I.
> *(The cleaner goes out onto the veranda.)*
> Did you see her?

Rachelle

> Who?

Betty

> The cleaning lady. Didn't you see her?

Rachelle

> I saw her. What about her?

Betty

> Didn't you see how she looked at us?

Rachelle

> No, I didn't notice anything. How did she look at us?

Betty

> She had this weird expression on her face…
> *(The cleaning lady enters the room from the veranda, collects some sheets and towels, and exits the room.)*
>
> Did you see that?

Rachelle

> She's not too happy. But I don't see why her expression has anything to do with us.

Betty

> She's angry. Suddenly she has to clean our room for us.

Rachelle

> That her job. And we came here on very short notice – we didn't make a reservation. So she was called in to clean at the last minute.

Betty

> Should we have given her a tip?

Rachelle

> People give tips when they leave.

Betty

> I think she was angry about the mess she found here.

Rachelle

> Is that our responsibility too? We are the ones who should be angry that they put us in a room like this.
> *(The phone rings. Betty picks up the receiver.)*

Betty

> Yes. What? Oh, reception. Yes. Who? A reporter? A reporter from the United States wants to talk to us? No. Sorry. No. Thanks.
> *(Hangs up the receiver.)*
>
> An American reporter wants to talk to us! We're famous! Maybe they really were looking for us!

Rachelle

> A reporter? From which newspaper?

Betty

> He didn't say.

Rachelle

> You could have said a word or two to the reporter. That we're alive and well.

Betty

> I don't want to speak to anybody. Especially not until we know where Susan is and what's happened to her.

Rachelle

> When we land in the States it won't be so easy to evade reporters.

Betty

> We'll see when we get there.

Rachelle

> And they'll ask about Susan.

Betty

> Is that what's worrying you? Their questions?

Rachelle

> No, I'm just saying…I'm just saying…there really wasn't much we could have done. I hope everything's fine. You said there weren't any risks involved.

Betty

> The leopard man. Do you remember him?

Rachelle

> Let's hope Susan and the leopard man didn't cross paths. She did say that she'd seen him once.

Betty

> Right. I think what she saw was a cat. If it'd actually been him…

Rachelle

> She said that she saw him from a distance, between some trees.

Betty

> It was in broad daylight, from far away. But what about at night, up close…if she saw him last night…I don't know…

Rachelle

> What would you say to the leopard man if you met him at night, alone, just you and him, a split second before he crushes your skull with a swift blow to the head?

Betty

> Am I supposed to say anything to him?

Rachelle

> You could. You don't have to. You wouldn't be able to overpower him.

Betty

> What could I possibly say to him?

Rachelle

> I don't know…you're not usually the one to keep quiet…

Betty

> I'd tell him, "We're exactly like you. Fighting for our territory."
> *(The phone rings. Betty picks up the receiver.)*

Hello. Yes. Yes. What? Vaccinations? What vaccinations? Sir, this is not the time to sell us vaccinations. We're leaving! We have no need for vaccinations.
(Hangs up the receiver.)

Rachelle

Let's go to sleep. We have a very busy day tomorrow. Imagine, sleeping on a bed! On a soft bed! After a shower! Aren't you excited?

Betty

Will anything we have done here remain with us?

Rachelle

Our friendship will survive. I'm certain about that. Our friendship will remain. Let's get some sleep.

Scene 6

In a field, not far from the forest. Gordon, carrying a backpack, and Sokol, a local man.

Gordon

> I'm hungry and thirsty. I never thought that this is what it would be like, being out here all alone. I thought I'd have to overcome anxiety, loneliness, struggle with dangerous animals, maybe even the leopard man—have you heard about him, about the leopard man? What? You don't understand, do you? I'm hungry. Is your village there? The village? There?

Sokol

> Village.

Gordon

> There?

Sokol

> Yes. There.

Gordon

> You don't have a compass by any chance, do you? According to the direction of the setting sun, north should be that way. *(Points into the distance.)*

But I have a feeling that it is not correct. Suddenly it seems to me that the sun is setting in the north. What do you think? Is the sun right?

Sokol

(*Points at Gordon's watch.*)

How much?

Gordon

The watch? You want to buy my watch?

Sokol

How much?

Gordon

I can't sell the watch to you. I need it.

Sokol

How much?

Gordon

No. No. It's not for sale. These cows, are they yours? The cows? Yours?

Sokol

Yes. The cows. Yes.

Gordon

Nice cows. Horns…big…horns.

Sokol

How much? The watch?

Gordon

No, I'm not going to sell it.

Sokol

This.

(*Points at a cow.*)

You want?

Gordon

> You want to give it to me? This calf? In return for the watch?
> No, thank you. What would I do with a calf? No, thank you.
> Are you returning to your village soon? To the village? The
> village. There.

Sokol

> There. Yes.

Gordon

> You're not returning? There?

Sokol

> Yes. There.

Gordon

> It will be dark soon. Are you staying? Staying here? You don't
> want to leave the cows here on their own... It's impossible
> to leave them here on their own ... I understand. It can be
> dangerous, to go alone. Of course I have this...
> *(Takes a knife out of his pocket.)*
>
> …but I don't know…

Sokol

> No. No. No good. This no good. This.

Gordon

> A knife? No good?

Sokol

> No. No good. This.
> *(Points at Gordon's watch).*
>
> This. Good.

Gordon

> No. It's not for sale.
> *(Leaves.)*

SCENE 7

Office of the President of the East African Republic. President Benzazi is talking on the telephone. Ramsey is in the room.

President

> (*Hangs up the receiver.*)
>
> Yes, Mr. Ramsey, what can I do for you?

Ramsey

> I'm about to leave your country, Mr. President, and you have helped me considerably. I wanted to thank you in person for everything you've done.

President

> The pleasure was all mine. Why are you leaving? Has something happened?

Ramsey

> No, nothing's happened. I'm missing home, my wife, my boys. That's all. I've been here for six years—six and a half, to be exact.

President

> And has it been long enough?

Ramsey

> Yes, it has. Not that I'm complaining, but…

President

Has your stay been enjoyable?

Ramsey

Yes, certainly. But it's time for me to be getting home. Of course I would love to have the opportunity to visit here again.

President

So all in all your time here can be summed up positively. You received several licenses and information that local business people didn't always have access to.

Ramsey

I said I have nothing to complain about.

President

You organized a safari for journalists in several reserves. You also took quite a long trip with a certain female reporter, if my memory serves me well.

Ramsey

You don't miss a thing, Mr. President. It was an organized trip for the journalists, but they didn't show up, so she stayed…

President

You also wrote several guide books about the reserves. You earned a bit from that.

Ramsey

True. But oddly enough I didn't earn much.

President

So you earned a small amount. That's also something. What are you planning to do at home, after resting a bit, of course?

Ramsey

> I have a few plans. What I'd really like to do is write. And I have plenty to say.

President

> Memoirs from the East African Republic?

Ramsey

> Yes. Mr. President, I wanted to ask you—do you feel safe?

President

> Safe?

Ramsey

> Do you feel safe?

President

> From what point of view?

Ramsey

> Mr. President, I travel quite a bit around your country, and I hear things. And not always…not always…

President

> What "not always"? Don't be afraid, Mr. Ramsey. You can speak freely.

Ramsey

> You're not well-liked in some places.

President

> Not well-liked? I'm not supposed to be well-liked.

Ramsey

> I've heard numerous calls to overthrow you, Mr. President.

President

> A revolution?

Ramsey

> Something like that.

President

> And in gratitude for what I have done for you, you are telling me... Good. But why are you telling me these things now, just before you leave the country?

Ramsey

> Because I'm meeting with you now. The truth is...

President

> I'm glad you're telling me these things now, and not by phone from New York. However, there's no need for concern.

Ramsey

> You're not concerned?

President

> You heard people talking. People talk everywhere. Or perhaps you heard something very specific?

Ramsey

> Nothing specific. Just people talking. But not just any talk. There's talk of your use of violence, arrests, torture, the murder of political opponents...

President

> Well, in order to maintain the government here it's necessary to implement all sorts of actions. We don't have hundreds of years of democratic tradition like you have in America or England.

Ramsey

> But people are talking...

President

> There's no cause for alarm. First of all you haven't heard those who support me. There are those who want me to continue, but you don't hear them.

Ramsey

The question is...the question is...

President

Believe me, Mr. Ramsey, I don't do more than what's necessary. But certain things have to be done. It's part of the regime. People here expect it. Without it they would think I was weak. Of course they complain. That's also part of it. Talking helps people let off steam.

Ramsey

Talk can turn into action, Mr. President.

President

I'm aware of that, but the army is loyal to me. Or is it? I don't know any more. Do you have any information about this?

Ramsey

About the army? No, nothing, sir. I didn't move in those circles.

President

I feel better...

Ramsey

Just because I wasn't there and didn't hear anything, doesn't mean that you don't have any reason to worry, Mr. President.

President

There is no reason to worry, Mr. Ramsey. Believe me, if I'd visited New York or Washington and heard complaints against your president, I would not even consider warning your president about a revolution, military or civil.

Ramsey

You forget, Mr. President, that there has already been a military coup here. That's how you came into power, isn't it?

President

> We were four officers who led the coup, then I took the reins of government—and believe me, Mr. Ramsey, conditions under the king prior to our current government were far worse than they are today. I divided up the land, established irrigation projects, built roads—the economic situation has definitely improved. I'm not even going to mention all the corruption that existed before I came into power. And we'll still return to democracy. I'm certain of that.

Ramsey

> There are foreign journalists here. They're reporting about things they're seeing and hearing.

President

> Violence exists everywhere. I don't think anyone is particularly interested in what's happening here. Even the story about the man in the leopard mask and his violent actions drew more attention, locally and abroad, than stories about my violent actions—that is, if any of these stories are true.

Ramsey

> If not for that man, the media would have been paying much more attention to you and your deeds.

President

> Perhaps.

Ramsey

> For your purposes, if the man in the leopard mask hadn't existed, would it have been necessary to invent him?

President

> It's possible. Someone has already hinted to me that perhaps I'm behind that crazy murderer.

Ramsey

> And are you, sir?

President

No! Never! Don't forget that there's another side to this as well. I'm getting complaints from all quarters about why we haven't yet succeeded in arresting the leopard man. What do I need this aggravation for?

Ramsey

Have you tried to arrest him?

President

Of course! He's dangerous. He murders little girls.

Ramsey

Do you have any information about his identity?

President

Who? The leopard man?

Ramsey

Yes.

President

I don't have a clue. We're not the only place with lunatics and murderers.

Ramsey

You're right, Mr. President, there are murderers everywhere. Not all, however, disguise themselves as a leopard. What's he trying to achieve by wearing this mask?

President

I don't know. Perhaps there's a certain need to be a beast. Have you ever heard of this need, Mr. Ramsey, of wanting to be a beast?

Ramsey

No, sir, I haven't.

President

> You know what they say—all's fair in love and war. Sometimes you want to be the evil beast, in both love and war, and he's waging a war against the entire world.

Ramsey

> Angry with everyone? Hates everybody?

President

> I don't know. It's hard to understand a man like this.

Ramsey

> Do you ever have the urge to be a beast, Mr. President?

President

> I assume it has happened to me too, Mr. Ramsey, just as it has to anyone else.

Ramsey

> Because there have been claims, Mr. President, as you yourself have hinted, that you may be behind this lunatic…

President

> I've hinted that I'm behind this crazy person?

Ramsey

> No, you hinted that there have been rumors to that effect.

President

> True. Have you heard anything along those lines?

Ramsey

> Yes, I've heard something.

President

> And do you believe what you heard, Mr. Ramsey?

Ramsey

> I don't think I have any reason to believe it, Mr. President.

President

> You don't sound so sure.

Ramsey

> I have no reason to believe that you're behind that man.

President

> I don't know how anyone can even think such a thing, Mr. Ramsey. To compare me to that lunatic? He kills left and right. He doesn't give a damn, doesn't think—he acts irrationally. I think, I check things. If I do anything ugly or unpleasant, it's the result of careful planning. I count to ten, and sometimes even to twenty, before I do something. How can you compare me to a lunatic like him?

Ramsey

> I'm not comparing. I'm just saying that I've heard talk about it.

President

> I'm not blaming you for what you've heard. I'm just saying that there's no logic behind these claims. But don't worry, Mr. Ramsey—he'll be caught sooner or later. Lunatics like him…

Ramsey

> He may be crazy, but he's very careful.

President

> Sooner or later he'll make a mistake. Do you know what I once thought about the man in the leopard skin? I thought how difficult it must be to wear the leopard skin. Think about him walking in the forest. The sun is bearing down on his head…

Ramsey

> I think he only wears the mask at night, sir, when he attacks.

President

> Not only at night, but mainly at night. That's true. But even at night it's pretty hot where he is. Here and there he approaches a village in the early evening and lies in wait for a little boy or girl playing alone outside. Once I imagined

how he goes toward a village, covered from head to toe in a leopard costume, slowly inching closer. The villagers are ready for him with arrows and spears, and suddenly he falls before he reaches the village . He gets up and falls again. The villagers run toward him and see that he cannot breathe inside his leopard costume. He tries to get up again, and boom! He falls. He gets up (The president spreads his arms.)

And he falls…

Ramsey

He's not totally covered by the leopard skin. Only the upper part of his body is covered.

President

Well…you've seen him, haven't you? You told me about it once.

Ramsey

Just for a few seconds, in very bad light…so…

President

I think you were very lucky. He entered your tent, didn't he?

Ramsey

I threatened him with a gun. That stopped him.

President

You drew a gun…

Ramsey

Yes.

President

Why didn't you shoot him?

Ramsey

If it had been a real leopard, which at first I thought it was, I wouldn't have hesitated. As soon as I realized that it wasn't a leopard, I couldn't shoot. It was a person. Plus he stopped the moment he saw the gun.

President

The gun frightened him?

Ramsey

I don't know. Apparently. Would you have shot him had it been you?

President

I would have shot, yes.

Ramsey

Don't you ever hesitate before you pull the trigger?

President

Depends on the circumstances. According to what you described, there is no room for hesitation. Now, if you will excuse me, Mr. Ramsey...

Ramsey

You usually don't hesitate, sir.

President

Sometime I do. But in some situations one should never hesitate. It's either you or him. So now, please excuse me...

Ramsey

Don't you regard him as a symbol, Mr. President?

President

A symbol? The man in the mask?

Ramsey

Some see him as representing something.

President

He's not a symbol. A symbol of what? I don't understand.

Ramsey

I don't really know...

President

> He's a symbol of nothing. Now…if you would please excuse me…

Ramsey

> (*Stands up.*)

> I would like to thank you for all the help you have offered me these past six and a half years, Mr. President.

President

> I was happy to do it. Don't hesitate to return if you miss us. (*Ramsey shakes the president's hand and turns to leave.*)

> I hope the next time you come for a visit, this lunatic will be safely behind bars.

Ramsey

> I hope so too, sir.
> (*Leaves.*)

Scene 8

Inside a hut in an African village. Susan is seated. A local villager is treating her ankle.

Susan

    Slowly. That hurts.

Villager

    I'm being careful…does it hurt here?

Susan

    Yes, yes. Here. No. Here.

Villager

    Where did this happen?

Susan

    Over there, in the forest. I left our cave and wandered a bit farther than usual. I was lost in thought. I suddenly noticed how far away from the cave I was, and that I didn't really know how to get back. I was a little confused, a little nervous, so I started to run because it was getting dark. I must have stumbled over something because I fell and passed out. When I woke up, it was morning—ouch! Don't touch there!

Villager

    I'm trying…

Susan

    Be careful, please!

Villager

Okay. I don't think it's broken. It's only sprained. I'll bandage it for you.

Susan

Gently, okay?

Villager

I'm just a paramedic, not a doctor, and I'm trying my best. Were you hurt when you fell?

Susan

Yes, I got banged up.

Villager

Your head, I mean.

Susan

Yes, I banged my head too, but it doesn't seem too serious. Not now, anyway. My head also hurt when I woke up, but the pain's gone. My leg hurts. I could barely manage to hobble to the village.

Villager

(Bandaging Susan's leg.)

Did you get something to eat?

Susan

Yes, yes…

Villager

Don't move your leg, ma'am.

Susan

My girlfriends are probably going crazy with worry wondering what could have happened to me. I'd like to get back to them as quickly as possible, to set their minds at ease. But I'm afraid…

Villager

That's it.
(Finishes bandaging Susan's ankle.)

Now you must rest. You can't walk on that leg for at least twenty-four hours, and even then you won't be able to walk without crutches.

Susan

I have to let my friends know somehow. They're probably worried sick.

Villager

Perhaps we can send someone there, to your cave.

Susan

Do you have any crutches I could use?
(Tries to stand up.)

Villager

No, ma'am, you mustn't walk!

Susan

Ouch!
(Sits down again.)

Villager

I've already told you, you mustn't walk! You must sit here. Don't move!

Susan

Fine. I won't move. Do you have something I could take for the pain?

Villager

I've already given you a painkiller. You don't need another one. You need to sit.

Susan

Do you have any Coca-Cola?

Villager

Coke? No, I don't think so.

Susan

Okay. Okay. Let's sit here. Where did you learn English?

Villager

We learn it here, in the region, at school, like they do anywhere in the world.

Susan

But not all the villagers here can speak English.

Villager

Not everyone goes to school. Not to a regular school, anyway.

Susan

You don't have Coke, you don't have Pepsi…

Villager

We don't have things like that here.
(Ozotto, a villager dressed in exotic clothes, approaches Susan and the villager.)

Ozotto

How are you?

Susan

Could be better, but…

Ozotto

Did he take good care of you?

Susan

No complaints. He's okay. Speaks English too.

Ozotto

How's the leg?

Susan

> Better.

Ozotto

> This morning I thought you'd pass out from the pain.

Susan

> It's much better now.

Villager

> I'm going now. If there's any problem, you know where to find me.

Susan

> Thank you.
> *(The villager says something in his own language and leaves.)*

Ozotto

> Did you get some food?

Susan

> I ate that…porridge.

Ozotto

> Would you like some more?

Susan

> No, thanks. It was good, but I've had enough. Really.

Ozotto

> Good. Get some rest. In the meantime I want to show you something.
> *(Leaves. Susan examines her ankle. Ozotto returns with a villager carrying a large drum. The villager starts beating his drum and Ozotto starts dancing.)*

Susan

> If my leg were better…believe me…I would join you.
> *(The drumming comes to an end and Ozotto stops dancing.)*

Ozotto

That's the dance we do before going out to hunt. Now I want to tell you a bit about our beliefs.

Susan

Your beliefs?

Ozotto

We believe that each tree, each bush, has its own soul. We also believe that every tree, every bush and every stone has a spirit, its own special god that guards it. Everything in this world has an independent existence, yet coexists with everything else in perfect harmony. When there's no harmony, there's a forest fire, war between people, between husband and wife, problems in our bodies. We also believe that we don't disappear after death. We continue being part of nature. Our souls continue living on the land, continue seeing, hearing, and being involved in everything. Our souls accompany our children and grandchildren wherever they go. Angering our souls can cause wars and arguments. One has to know how to honor the souls of the dead. Harmony is very important. We aren't always in a rush, like you are. We don't have objects, houses, or cars. We have time, space. One has to know how to live in peace with one's space and surroundings. To live in harmony with everything in nature. With what one sees as well as with what one doesn't see, but feels. We are truly part of the universe and always will be. Therefore we are not in a hurry to get anywhere.
(Starts singing. The drummer starts beating his drum.)

Susan

Excuse me, Ozotto.

Ozotto

I'm praying.
(Continues singing.)

Susan

Do you know what we Americans believe?

Ozotto

>I'm praying to the good spirits, asking them to accept us, guide us, show us the way.
>*(Continues singing.)*

Susan

>What I'm concerned about now is my friends in the cave.

Ozotto

>Usually tourists from Europe and America want to hear about these things.
>*(Sings a bit more, then stops.)*

Susan

>But most tourists don't break their legs and lose their friends. I'm sorry. What you told me is actually very interesting, really. But I have to go.

Ozotto

>You can't go. You must rest.

Susan

>I can hobble along.

Ozotto

>You can't even do that. Perhaps tomorrow morning we can arrange a car to take you to the cave.

Susan

>And in the meantime...

Ozotto

>In the meantime you'll rest.

Susan

>But I don't know what my friends must be thinking. I'm sure they're very worried about me.

Ozotto

>It's not possible for you to see them today. I hope I can arrange a car for tomorrow morning.

Susan

Are you a witchdoctor?

Ozotto

I'm not a doctor. This is our tribe's traditional dress.

Susan

But you don't dress like this all the time, do you?

Ozotto

No, not every day. Only for special occasions and holidays.

Susan

And you wore it especially for me?

Ozotto

Not just for you…

Susan

For the tourists.

Ozotto

I speak English, so I was asked to explain our beliefs to the tourists.

Susan

You already know what tourists what to hear…

Ozotto

Everything I told you is absolutely true. I didn't invent a thing.

Susan

Are you a shaman?

Ozotto

Only for the tourists.

Susan

Do you at least earn something by doing this?

Ozotto

> Sometimes, here and there. Didn't you bring any colored beads?

Susan

> I don't have anything with me.

Ozotto

> Glass beads? A broken mirror? Anything?

Susan

> No, nothing,
> *(The drummer starts pounding the drum. Ozotto signals him to stop. He continues. Ozotto approaches him and again signals him to stop. He stops.)*
>
> I really don't have anything here with me.

Ozotto

> That's okay. I'll do it for nothing. Our traditions are very important to us, and presenting them to tourists preserves our beliefs for generations to come. Without the tourists…

Susan

> You love it.

Ozotto

> It's important. Without tourists, I doubt anyone would do it.

Susan

> Don't they believe in it?

Ozotto

> They do, but they don't practice it anymore. Perhaps once or twice a year.
> *(A local man enters with Gordon.)*

Susan

> Who's that?

Gordon

> I'm Gordon. Who are you?

Susan

> I'm Susan.

Gordon

> I was told that there was a white woman here.

Ozotto

> Who are you?
> (*The local man leaves.*)

Gordon

> I've been wandering around this area since this morning. A friend brought me here, not far from here…and…

Susan

> Are you British?

Gordon

> Yes, and you're American?

Ozotto

> Are you traveling around here alone?

Gordon

> A friend brought me…an American.

Ozotto

> Are you a tourist or on some official business?

Gordon

> Tourist. A regular tourist.

Ozotto

> And where is this American friend who brought you here?

Gordon

> He returned to Abilda. Why?

Ozotto

So you are here on your own, just like that.

Gordon

Why? Is it dangerous?

Ozotto

It can be. And why did he leave you here alone like this?

Gordon

He wanted to stay in the car and I wanted to go for a walk. That's how it happened.

Susan

What happened?

Gordon

I told him I wanted to walk around a bit in the area and we arranged to meet at a certain time and place. We decided that if we didn't find each other then, I'd make my own way back to Abilda. In the end we didn't meet. I presume he has gone back.

Susan

Perhaps he's looking for you.

Gordon

I don't think so. We decided that he wouldn't wait for me too long.

Ozotto

So he left you on your own.

Gordon

There's a bus back to town, isn't there?

Ozotto

And in the meantime you're wandering around here alone.

Gordon

I wanted to learn about the tribe…

Susan

You got lost, didn't you?

Gordon

You could say that…

Ozotto

Just this morning they let some animals out of the reserve and there may be some predators among them. Did you see any?

Gordon

I didn't see any animals.

Susan

Nor did I. When I woke up this morning, I didn't see any particular animal.

Ozotto

What do you mean you didn't see any particular animal?

Susan

I didn't see any animals nearby. I saw something from a distance, but nothing clearly. It may have been a tree…or…

Gordon

Why did they let the animals out of the reserve? I understand that this village is not part of the reserve.

Ozotto

No. It is not.

Gordon

So why did they let the animal…

Ozotto

They do so from time to time.

Gordon

For hunting purposes? I understand hunting is prohibited in the reserves.

Ozotto

No. It's part of the reserve authority policy to thin the animal population, to maintain a balance. Or so they said. But in any case, it's dangerous to wander around here alone.

Gordon

What's the danger?

Ozotto

Not everyone here is friendly. You may see someone walking toward you, even smiling at you, but he may have a knife in his pocket.

Gordon

Are you thinking of anyone in particular?

Ozotto

No. But not everyone likes strangers.

Susan

Whites…

Gordon

(To Susan.)

How did you end up here? What's your name?

Susan

Susan. I came here with two friends, also Americans, and we're living in a cave not far from here. Yesterday evening I left the cave alone and got lost. I started to run and fell. I sprained my ankle.

Gordon

A cave? You've been living in a cave?

Susan

Yes.

Gordon

Why in a cave?

Susan

> We wanted to see if we could survive in a place like that. We've been there for over two months. Anyway, I fell, passed out, and woke up this morning.

Gordon

> You woke up just like that, in the bush?

Susan

> Yes.

Ozotto

> And you saw no animals?

Susan

> No. I woke up and saw that I wasn't far from the village, so I limped here. It's interesting that the pain only started when I got here.

Gordon

> And now you can't get back to your cave with your injured ankle...

Susan

> No.

Gordon

> Maybe they'll be looking for you.

Susan

> Where will they look? There are several villages in the area. How would they know that I'm in this one?

Ozotto

> They'll eventually pass through here and ask about you. Don't worry.

Gordon

> So how did you manage in the cave?

Susan

> We managed.

Gordon

> Alone? Without any help?

Susan

> Yes, you could say that.

Gordon

> What did you eat?

Susan

> Whatever we found. We cooked rats.

Gordon

> Rats?

Susan

> Yes. And rabbits.

Ozotto

> Rabbits? Here?

Susan

> We called them rabbits. I don't know. It looks like a big—

Gordon

> And that's what you came for? All the way from the United States?

Susan

> Not exactly, but when we arrived, we decided to try it.

Ozotto

> The main thing is that you're alive and well. And now…

Susan

> You're praying to the good spirits…

Ozotto

> The main thing is that you're healthy, because now…
> *(A local women approaches Susan, Ozotto, the drummer, and Gordon with a pot, places it off to the side, and leaves. The drummer follows her out.)*
> Would you like to eat?

Gordon

> I wouldn't mind something to eat.
> *(A second woman approaches with a pot, puts it down, and leaves.)*
> It seems we have enough here.

Ozotto

> Eat, eat. The lady has already eaten.

Gordon

> I've also already eaten.
> *(Peeks into a pot.)*
> What do you call this dish?

Ozotto

> *(Looks into the pot.)*
> *I don't know if the name will mean anything to you, but help yourself. It's tasty.*
> *(A third woman enters, puts down a pot, and leaves.)*

Gordon

> We have plenty. Thanks.

Susan

> Just be careful. It's spicy. I can tell. I ate—

Gordon

> When you're hungry, you can eat anything.

Ozotto

> Eat. It's good. I'll leave you now. Susan, you'll sleep here, and Gordon,

(Turns to Gordon)

you'll sleep in another hut. Look for me when you've finished eating. My name is Ozotto, everyone knows where I live, and I'll show you where you can sleep. In the meantime, eat. Perhaps you two have something to discuss. You both got lost…
(Leaves.)

Gordon

They didn't leave us any plates or cutlery.

Susan

There's something here. This is what I used.
(Passes him a fork.)

Gordon

You ate with this.

Susan

Yes.
(Takes a jar of water and washes the fork.)

Gordon

Okay, let's see…
(Takes the fork and starts eating.)

Wow! It's hot!

Susan

I told you!

Gordon

Could you give me something to drink?
(Susan passes him the jar and he takes a sip.)

What's in this pot?
(Examines it, then eats.)

This isn't very tasty, but…

Susan

When you're hungry…

Gordon

And thirsty…
(Drinks from the jar.)

How long were you in this cave for?

Susan

I told you. Over two months.

Gordon

And what did you do there, besides eat rats?

Susan

We survived. We learned to live under harsh conditions. That's about it.

Gordon

Whose idea was it? Who paid for it?

Susan

Nobody paid for it.

Gordon

Did *National Geographic* subsidize the project?

Susan

No. It wasn't subsidized by anyone.
(Gordon pushes away the pot, peeks into another one, and decides against it. He sips some water.)

Gordon

And did you learn how to survive?

Susan

We survived.

Gordon

It would be interesting to visit your cave.

Susan

> Come tomorrow. Ozotto, the man who just left, said he'd arrange a car to take me tomorrow.

Gordon

> And your friends, do they know you're here?

Susan

> No, and they're not aware that animals have been released into this area. Perhaps predatory animals too.

Gordon

> Well, you wanted to survive. How many friends do you have there?

Susan

> Two. Betty and Rachelle.

Gordon

> Betty and Rachelle. From America. Did you get along? The three of you, I mean?

Susan

> Very well. Why shouldn't we? We're friends.

Gordon

> That may be, but living together, especially under these harsh conditions…

Susan

> There's some occasional friction. There are arguments sometimes, but in general…

Gordon

> You got on well.

Susan

> Yes. What are you doing in these parts?

Gordon

> I'm just a tourist…

Susan

Wandering around here alone…you got lost…

Gordon

I didn't get lost.

Susan

So what are you doing here?

Gordon

What any tourist does here. I wanted to see some animals. The local people.

Susan

So why didn't you take a guided tour like everyone else?

Gordon

I'm not a fan of guided tours.

Susan

You're taking a risk. Alone, in a place like this…

Gordon

I have a knife.
(Points to his bag.)

Susan

You're not a regular tourist. For some reason…

Gordon

Neither are you. Or your friends.

Susan

But I told you—we wanted to challenge ourselves to see if we could live completely cut off from the world. And you, you aren't telling…

Gordon

I was looking for something. But why does it matter?

Susan

> And did you find what you were looking for?

Gordon

> No, not yet. Why is it important?

Susan

> It's not. It's just interesting. Do you want to come with me to our cave tomorrow? To see how we live there?

Gordon

> Yes.

Susan

> Then, maybe, when we'll get there, you'll tell us what you're really looking for?

Gordon

> Perhaps. So how is your leg?

Susan

> It's better now. This morning…
> *(Ozotto enters with a local.)*

Ozotto

> Miss Susan, this man
> *(Points to the local.)*
>
> claims that this morning he saw two white women at the bus station. He claims that the army brought them there this morning, and that apparently they got on the bus. He says they were more or less the same age as you. With bags. Perhaps these were your friends?

Susan

> Why should these two women be my friends? Perhaps they were just two more tourists traveling around this area?

Ozotto

> There aren't usually tourists around here. Tourists usually go to the reserve, which is several kilometers south of here.

Susan

And soldiers brought them to the bus station?

Ozotto

Yes, according to this man.

Susan

Why would the army take them to the bus station? Were they told they had to leave.?

Ozotto

I don't know. Perhaps it's forbidden to be in the cave?

Susan

Is this a military zone?

Ozotto

I don't think so. Perhaps it's because of the animals they brought here from the reserve. In fact, I remember that someone was wandering around here with some soldiers, warning people.

Susan

Does the army deal with things like this?

Ozotto

Sometimes.

Susan

What did the two women look like? What were they wearing?

Ozotto

(Exchanges a few words with the local man.)

One of them, the taller one, was blond.
(The local says something.)

Or at least she had lighter hair, anyway.

Susan

What were they wearing?

Ozotto

> (*Exchanges a few words with the local man.*)

> He can only remember that one of them was wearing a green dress. He doesn't remember which one.
> (*The local man says something to Ozotto.*)

> He says he remembers a brown bag, with white stripes.

Susan

> Then it really was them. Rachelle has a bag like that. A large one. We always said that if a lion came into the cave, she could always get in that bag and zip it shut. The lion would never know she was there. The army brought them to the bus station?

Ozotto

> That's what he said.

Susan

> It's them, it's them. Fine. So they left the cave. But I still have to get back there, I've got all sorts of things there. My passport...

Ozotto

> Tomorrow. You'll think about it tomorrow. I just hope that while you were away, a leopard or some other animal hasn't moved in. We'll discuss it tomorrow.
> (*Leaves with the local.*)

Susan

> I need my passport, clothes, and money.

Gordon

> Are you determined to go back no matter what?

Susan

> I need my passport. But at the same time, the thought of hobbling all the way there...I don't know...

Gordon

Even if you don't go back for your passport, I'm sure the American embassy will help you.

Susan

And you won't help me?

Gordon

I'll help you, I'll help you. If necessary.

Susan

Perhaps one day I'll be able to return the favor, when I know what you're looking for.

Gordon

Perhaps.
(Stands up.)

I'm going. Aren't you afraid of sleeping here in the hut alone?

Susan

No. Why should I be afraid?

Gordon

A white woman…alone…

Susan

These people are okay. At least that's what I want to believe.

Gordon

All of them?

Susan

I don't know all of them, but they seem okay.

Gordon

I will nevertheless sleep with my knife under the pillow.

Susan

> I don't have a knife.

Gordon

> See you tomorrow.
> *(Leaves)*

SCENE 9

Akilla's office in the Foreign Ministry at night. Akilla and Dabbon are sitting in the office.

Akilla

> I told you not to come to my office so late. It looks suspicious. During regular working hours is better.

Dabbon

> I didn't understand what you were trying to tell me on the phone.

Akilla

> That's because I can't speak openly on the phone. We're being listened to, Dabbon! But you should be able to understand a hint!

Dabbon

> So I didn't understand! So what! So can't we talk? Can't we meet?

Akilla

> No! Not now, no! Dabbon, you are putting me at risk, you are putting yourself at risk! I hope this office isn't bugged!

Dabbon

> I understand that the coup has been delayed yet again!

Akilla

> Correct!

Dabbon

> For how long?

Akilla

> A month, perhaps a month and a half. The army is moving now, training, about to do something that wasn't previously planned.

Dabbon

> Is that what Bono Kali told you?

Akilla

> Yes.

Dabbon

> A month and a half…

Akilla

> That's what he says. But the truth is, we are not prepared yet.

Dabbon

> Why aren't we prepared?

Akilla

> Because not everything is in place yet. There are still things to do. There are some things you don't know.

Dabbon

> I do know that we keep putting it off…

Akilla

> Sometimes we have no choice, Dabbon. It's better to be well prepared and not to make mistakes.

Dabbon

> We've postponed it several time. That was our mistake. If we hadn't delayed it, the army's current orders wouldn't be a problem, because the coup would have been behind us by now.

Akilla

You talk as if a coup is such an easy and simple matter...

Dabbon

How is it that our colonel was not aware of these orders?

Akilla

I told you. Nobody knew about these orders in advance. He's just a colonel, Bono Kali. He doesn't know everything.

Dabbon

Perhaps the president decided to make this move because he suspects something?

Akilla

Perhaps. We don't know. Whatever the case, Dabbon, I want you to know that a coup is not a matter to be taken lightly. It's not an easy thing to do. One has to be prepared to shoot innocents, regular soldiers who are simply carrying out their orders. My impression of Bono Kali is that he's cautious, and that's good. It's good to hesitate before giving the order to shoot—sometimes to shoot your own people. You sit here and talk, but somebody has to do the shooting.

Dabbon

To shoot the president! Nobody else! Perhaps not even him! That would be enough…

Akilla

And perhaps it's necessary to shoot him! And not just him! He has bodyguards and numerous admirers everywhere. There could be fighting.

Dabbon

So let's postpone it for another twenty years!

Akilla

Not twenty, but for the time being the issue is on hold, but not for too long. And you're right. It may be that the decision to move the army now, is because of the president's suspicions. And specifically for this reason we won't be meeting, other than for official matters. No meetings outside of work-related issues for the time being. And don't mention anything when speaking on the phone, not even the slightest hint of a coup.

Dabbon

We're going underground.

Akilla

Right. We've always been underground, but now…

Dabbon

Well…what can I say…by the way, the Englishman's wife, the one you asked me to entertain, called me from England. Her name is Lia. She was looking for him. Did she call you too?

Akilla

No. What happened? What did she want?

Dabbon

She wanted to know what's going on with her husband.

Akilla

What is going on with him?

Dabbon

He went on a trip to one of the reserves. So I heard. But I didn't hear exactly where. She called his hotel beforehand and they also couldn't tell her exactly where he is. So she started to worry. That's it.

Akilla

Why is she worried?

Dabbon

He also told her what he told us, that he wanted to see the man in the leopard mask. That's what's worrying her.

Akilla

And you don't know where he is?

Dabbon

No.

Akilla

Didn't I ask you to entertain him?

Dabbon

Yes, but I can't follow him twenty-four hours a day. Yesterday—

Akilla

How did she get to you?

Dabbon

Through his hotel. Don't you remember? They informed us of his arrival. And of course they saw us with him there when he arrived.

Akilla

They didn't see us with him, but they knew that we were waiting in his room. What did you tell her? Did you allay her fears?

Dabbon

Yes. I told her there was nothing to worry about, that he has taken a trip and that he'd probably be back in a few days.

Akilla

Did she calm down?

Dabbon

I'm not sure. I tried to calm her down, but I don't know if there's any reason to remain calm. I made inquiries and was told that he went to one of the reserves with a man named Ramsey. Do you know him? I think he's well-known around here.

Akilla

> Yes. I think I know who he is. An American. If it's the person I'm thinking of, there's no need to worry. He's under the president's patronage.

Dabbon

> There's no need to worry about whom?

Akilla

> There's no need to worry about the Englishman. The president knows and supports this American, Ramsey.

Dabbon

> I've heard that he's quite an adventurer, this man.

Akilla

> Perhaps. But he isn't one to do anything stupid. By the way, the Englishman won't be seeing the man in the leopard mask. Did you hear the news this morning?

Dabbon

> No, I didn't.

Akilla

> Didn't you hear? They found the body of the man in the leopard mask.

Dabbon

> Found the body? Is he dead?

Akilla

> Yes, he's dead.

Dabbon

> Where did they find him?

Akilla

> Actually near the reserve we enlarged, the one we took the animals from. That *you* took the animals from. That's where they found him.

Dabbon

How do they know it's him?

Akilla

The body was mutilated, in pieces, and the leopard skin was next to it. They assume it's him.

Dabbon

A leopard skin? Perhaps someone killed a leopard and they found…

Akilla

I understand that it wasn't the remains of a leopard, but rather the actual skin that was worn by the person whose body they found.

Dabbon

Maybe it was someone else, another man wearing a leopard skin.

Akilla

They aren't certain it's him, but they're assuming it must be him. The nearby tribe, the Horai, they didn't report anyone missing, so I'm told. Therefore it must have been a stranger who was found with the leopard skin. So it seems…

Dabbon

Perhaps he was wandering around there and didn't know they were letting animals out. And we let out some predators too, as agreed. Perhaps he knew the area and thought he was safe, as usually there are no predators there. He was probably attacked suddenly by animals while lurking around the villages, looking for people to kill.

Akilla

Could be. So at least we did one good deed.

Dabbon

A good deed? I don' know. The president will take all the credit. In a way, he was a symbol of our revolution.

Akilla

> A symbol? Of the revolution? Who? The man in the leopard mask?

Dabbon

> Yes. He represented rebellion, freedom, nature…

Akilla

> He was an insane murderer. What's the matter with you?

Dabbon

> At least he wasn't afraid. We're sitting and waiting for the opportunity to act…

Akilla

> So what? I don't understand. He's a murderer. What does he have to be afraid of? Of murdering? Crazy murderers have no fear. Besides, maybe he's dead now because he wasn't afraid. We're alive and we have a coup to carry out. In any case, from now and until further notice we have to keep a lower profile, We have to—

Dabbon

> To keep a lower profile…

Akilla

> Yes. Absolutely.

Dabbon

> For how long?

Akilla

> For as long as necessary. I'll be in touch. And until then, don't initiate any contact with me. Is that clear?

Dabbon

> Yes.
> *(Leaves.)*

Scene 10

A road in the Raizer Reserve area. Enter Gordon, supporting Susan, who is limping.

Susan

> Let's sit down on that stone over there.

Gordon

> All right. Are you in pain?

Susan

> Yes. It's bearable, but I could use a rest.

Gordon

> So could I, though the bus station isn't too far away. I can see it from here.

Susan

> Come on. Let's sit.

Gordon

> Will you be able to make it to the bus station?

Susan

> Let's get to this stone first…

Gordon

> And yesterday you thought you'd be able to walk to the cave.

Susan

> I know, but I couldn't imagine that my leg would hurt so much. Besides, there are probably wild animals roaming around there by now.

Gordon

> I have a knife.

Susan

> We wouldn't find anything there anyway. The animals have probably eaten my passport.

Gordon

> I would have gone on my own. You could have waited for me in the village.

Susan

> After you help me to the capital, to the embassy, you can come back here.

Gordon

> I also wanted to see the cave.

Susan

> You can come back here when they round up all the predators. Here we go. Give me a hand?
> *(Susan sits on the stone.)*
>
> Come and sit down.

Gordon

> No, it's okay. I can stand. First see a doctor, then go to the embassy.

Susan

> I need papers. And money. But I'll see a doctor too.

Gordon

> Perhaps your friends took your papers with them.

Susan

We'll find that out at the embassy too. I'm certain they'll go there as well.

Gordon

I promised I'd help you. And I will.

Susan

I hope I'll be able to pay you back what it costs for this journey.

Gordon

It's nothing…

Susan

I want to repay you.

Gordon

Allow me to feel a bit like a knight in shining armor who saves the white damsel alone in the jungle...

Susan

You certainly have helped me, and it's extremely gallant of you. After all, you wanted to wander around this area a while, and now you're being forced to return to the city already.

Gordon

I'm happy to be of assistance. How are you going to find your friends if the embassy doesn't know where they are?

Susan

The embassy should at least be able to point me in the right direction.

Gordon

And what if you don't find them, despite all your efforts?

Susan

I don't know. I'll go to the hotel, have a good shower…

Gordon

> How did you manage to wash in the cave?

Susan

> There's a stream not far from there, but we didn't have bathing cuits and in daylight the local people would spy on us. We bathed in our underwear, and even so it wasn't pleasant being stared at. At night it was a bit scary to go there. So we didn't wash every day. Our clothes also needed to be washedevery now and then. We didn't do that too often either.

Gordon

> Did you have soap?
> *(Susan doesn't answer.)*
>
> Did you have any soap?

Susan

> Not really. We didn't have a lot of things. Do you have any idea what it's like to light a fire without any matches? Have you ever tried it?

Gordon

> Not that I can remember. Perhaps when I was a scout once. But it must have been an interesting experience, right? New experiences every day.

Susan

> Betty would tell us about her arguments with her husband, her problems with her children, and then urge us to talk about our problems at home. Rachelle shared a bit with us. I didn't feel comfortable with this, so I didn't tell them anything. It seemed like gossip to me. Is that what we came all this way to do? To talk about home?

Gordon

> And you waited for Tarzan. So you told me.

Susan

> Betty waited for him. The truth is, we were all waiting for something to happen. What did we come here for if nothing was going to happen?

Gordon

> What, for example?

Susan

> I don't know. Perhaps a delegation of anthropologists passing through with bundles balanced on their heads. And someone in a pith helmet saying, "Miss Betty, I presume." But nothing ever happened.

Gordon

> What about the tribe close by? Didn't anyone from there ever visit you?

Susan

> No. No one took any interest in us other than to spy on us while we bathed. Once an American with a Landrover took Betty for a drive.

Gordon

> An American? With a Landrover? Was it a yellow one perhaps?

Susan

> I don't remember.

Gordon

> Do you remember his name?

Susan

> No.

Gordon

> Was it Ramsey, by any chance?

Susan

> I don't remember. Anyway, he took her for a drive around the reserve, but they returned a few minutes later. She got out of the Landrover without saying a word, and he drove off.

Gordon

> He brought her back quickly?

Susan

> Yes.

Gordon

> What happened?

Susan

> I don't know. She didn't speak about it. I think that, as usual, she started giving him instructions, and he probably didn't like it.

Gordon

> Did he say anything?

Susan

> No. Not that I remember.

Gordon

> What was he doing near your cave?

Susan

> I don't really remember that either. I just remember that he was nearby, with his Landrover, talking about how he would like to help us. Betty mentioned something about us not being allowed into the reserve, just for the sake of saying something, and he offered to take her for a drive inside there.

Gordon

> Didn't she give any explanation afterward about what happened?

Susan

> She sort of hinted that he made a pass at her, but it wasn't very convincing. I think she was just looking for an excuse.

Gordon

> Why didn't it sound convincing? Couldn't it be that he tried to start with her?

Susan

> Could be. But then she would have gone on about it and not just hinted at something.

Gordon

> Perhaps she made a pass at him?

Susan

> And that's why be brought her back? I don't think so.

Gordon

> And Tarzan didn't come…

Susan

> No. He apparently preferred sitting at home with his wife, drinking tea.

Gordon

> He's an Englishman.

Susan

> What about you?

Gordon

> I'm an Englishman too.

Susan

> No, I mean about you coming out here looking for something.

Gordon

> Looking for something?

Susan

That's what you told me yesterday.

Gordon

True. I did.

Susan

So, what is it?

Gordon

I wanted to see the man in the leopard mask. Have you heard about him?

Susan

Yes, I've heard about him.

Gordon

I wanted to see him. Close up. To look into his eyes, face to face.

Susan

Why?

Gordon

It's hard for me to explain. I just want to, simple as that.

Susan

Isn't it dangerous?

Gordon

There's a certain risk involved. But I'm very cautious. I have a knife.

Susan

You want to see him face to face?

Gordon

Yes.

Susan

> But what will you see there? A mask made from leopard skin? What's to see there?

Gordon

> His eyes! The eyes!

Susan

> What do you expect to see in his eyes?

Gordon

> That's what I don't know. That's exactly what I want to find out.

Susan

> I'm afraid you'd be very disappointed.

Gordon

> Why do you say that?

Susan

> I saw him. I know.

Gordon

> You saw him? When?

Susan

> Several weeks ago.
>
> *(A local man enters with a little girl. He approaches Susan and Gordon, says something in the local language, points in the direction of the bus station, and tries to lift Gordon't bag. Gordon objects. The local continues pointing toward the bus station and tries to take Gordon's bag. Gordon doesn't allow it. The local concedes and leaves. The little girl approaches them and extends her hand to ask for charity. Susan gestures that she doesn't have anything. The girl insists. Susan gestures again that she doesn't have anything. The girl takes her hand back and turns to leave. The local enters and leads her away.)*

Susan

Why didn't you give her something?

Gordon

Why should I give her anything?

Susan

Why not? You have money, and you could have given her something.

Gordon

I don't like the way they use their children to beg. You should see what it's like in the capital. They cling to you, begging for money. They teach them to do it. To beg. I've given plenty. And I don't have loads of money.

Susan

It's not just the money, it's something to show her friends, a sort of memento, something they can play with. For her your coin is something…something…

Gordon

A memento?

Susan

To show off to her friends.

Gordon

I'm not sure about that, but perhaps you're right. So, you saw the man in the leopard mask Where?

Susan

I was walking in a part of the forest that seemed denser than usual. Suddenly I saw a man dressed in a leopard skin not far from me, around fifty yardsaway, perhaps less. At first I was terrified. He really does look like a leopard. Even his hands were covered in leopard skin, as if he were wearing gloves. But I quickly realized it was a human, a person. I could tell from his legs. They were not covered.

Gordon

Around fifty…fifty…

Susan

Yards. Yes.

Gordon

Were you frightened?

Susan

Absolutely! Wouldn't you be afraid if you saw a leopard standing nearby? But then I calmed down. I also remembered that there were no animals in the area. Certainly not predators.

Gordon

So you calmed down?

Susan

Absolutely.

Gordon

You saw the man in the leopard mask and you were able to calm down?

Susan

The moment I realized it was a person and not an animal, I relaxed. I wasn't even thinking of the masked man.

Gordon

What did you think at the time?

Susan

I thought he might be someone from a neighboring tribe. They dress up in all sorts of apparel. Preparing some ceremony, maybe. They have a variety of rites and dances.

Gordon

And then what happened?

Susan

> I stood still. I didn't know what to do. Even though it was a person and not an animal, it wasn't a pleasant feeling at all. There I was, alone, with a tribesman dressed in a pretty frightening costume. Suddenly he disappeared. That also spooked me. Then I saw him peering at me from behind a tree. I saw the palm of his hand on the tree and his head peering out at me and then he disappeared again behind the tree. Like he was playing hide-and-seek with me. As if he were beckoning me—"Come hither, I have a surprise for you!" Something like that.

Gordon

> Was he black?

Susan

> I think so.

Gordon

> You think so? Aren't you sure?

Susan

> I couldn't see that well.

Gordon

> You mentioned that you saw his legs.

Susan

> True. I did. But I don't remember exactly. I seem to remember his shoes more than I do his legs. But I don't remember thinking that he wasn't black. Who on earth would stand there dressed as a leopard besides a tribesman?

Gordon

> Aha. And then what happened?

Susan

> I turned around and moved away. It was not a pleasant experience, a little scary too.

Gordon

Didn't it enter your mind that it was the murderer in the leopard mask?

Susan

No, not at the time. I only thought of it afterward. Even now I'm not sure. If it was him, why didn't he kill me?

Gordon

Perhaps you surprised him. He wasn't prepared for it.

Susan

Maybe.

Gordon

So what did you do?

Susan

I told you. I turned around and moved away.

Gordon

Did you notice if he followed you?

Susan

I didn't. I turned around twice or maybe three times but I didn't see him. I was actually feeling very uncomfortable about not engaging in his invitation to play hide-and-seek. It was as if he were saying, "Come find me. Why are you running away? I'm a good person, I won't harm you. I just want to play." But I sensed something eerie in this game. A bit threatening.

Gordon

But you had heard of this masked man who murders people?

Susan

Yes. Of course. We were terrified of him.

Gordon

Nevertheless you didn't think…

Susan

I didn't think of anything. I simply ran away and returned to the cave.

Gordon

Did he have a weapon in his hand? A knife?

Susan

I didn't see anything.

Gordon

Were you armed?

Susan

I had a pointed stick, nothing substantial. I find it hard to believe he would feel threatened by it.

Gordon

Nevertheless he hid from you.

Susan

It was like a game. He hid and I was supposed to find him. Hide-and-seek.

Gordon

What did your friends have to say about all of this? Hey! Look! The bus!

Susan

It's not going in the right direction, but it will return in half an hour. We'll get on then.

Gordon

So what did your friends say?

Susan

They didn't know what to say. From the little they did say, I don't think they really believed me entirely. But they also knew that I had no reason to lie. Anyway, that night we blocked the cave entrance with a particularly large pile of logs, which we lit on fire. We also took turns guarding the entrance.

Gordon

To be on the safe side?

Susan

Yes. But after a few days things went back to normal.

Gordon

Did you ever visit the tribe, see their ceremonies?

Susan

Only from a distance. Although this shaman, Ozotto, the one who helped us earlier, said that they rarely hold these rites anymore. I saw them.

Gordon

You startled him, the masked man. He's used to waylaying people, pouncing on them, and suddenly you came out of…

Susan

Could be. He didn't look startled. But I actually couldn't see his face. You might be right.

Gordon

So that's it? With time you just forgot about the whole episode?

Susan

Yes. At first we didn't dare venture out alone into the jungle or to the spring. Until the fear passed. But even then…

Gordon

Have you ever thought about what might have happened had you carried on walking without suspecting anything?

Susan

I have, but I don't have an answer.

Gordon

I think you were extremely lucky. Had you approached him…

Susan

What would you have done in my place?

Gordon

I would have inched closer toward him. I also would have drawn my knife. Just in case.

Susan

And if he attacked you with a knife in his hands?

Gordon

If I had enough space and time, I would have fled and climbed a tree. If not, I would have fought back with my knife. I want to see him, but I want to live more.

Susan

Do you intend to come back to these parts after abringing me back to the capital, to try and see this man? To look him in the eye?

Gordon

I think so.

Susan

And do you believe that you'll just be walking along and suddenly see him?

Gordon

I'm not so sure. But I'll take my chances. I'm not at all sure. I heard he's someone suffering from a terminal disease. If this is so, there's no guarantee that he's still alive. Would you like something to drink?

(Gordon takes a bottle out of his bag.)

Susan

> Yes.
> *(Gordon passes the bottle to her, she takes a sip and returns it to him. He also takes a sip.)*
>
> Terminally ill?

Gordon

> That's what they say. Mentally and terminally ill, an escapee from a mental institution.

Susan

> Where did you hear this?

Gordon

> In the capital. When I arrived.

Susan

> He didn't look as if he was dying…but you never know. Maybe the mask is hiding something.

Gordon

> Perhaps he didn't have the energy to chase and attack you.
> *(Two locals pass on their way to the bus station.)*

Susan

> And you think that's why he was hiding? Because he didn't have the energy?

Gordon

> I have no idea.

Susan

> I doubt you'll ever get to see him alive. He's a vicious and dangerous murderer. You'll never see him without his mask if he doesn't want you to. Maybe you'll get to see him dead, lying sprawled in the forest. But alive…

Gordon

> Lying dead? Do you think there'd be anything left after the animals finished with him?

Susan

> Maybe it's where there aren't any animals. Or no predators. If you saw him just lying there, still, at night, his face and the mask partially lit by moonlight—would you approach him? Would you remove the mask? After you're certain he's dead, I mean.

Gordon

> How would I know he's dead? He could be asleep.

Susan

> You could inch toward him very slowly.

Gordon

> It could be a trap. Perhaps he's only pretending to be asleep.

Susan

> Really, what would you do if you saw him sprawled on the ground in the forest?

Gordon

> Even if he was sleeping and not dead, I wouldn't go near him. I'd let him sleep in peace.

Susan

> You're saying that even crazy murderers deserve to sleep in peace?

Gordon

> If he's sleeping, then let him sleep. If he's dead…I don't want to see what's left of him. I came to see his eyes, alive.

Susan

> In any case, you eventually have to look your wife in the eye.

Gordon

> What's that got to do with it? I don't understand.

Susan

> This morning you told me that you're having problems with your wife.

Gordon

> True. But what's the connection?

Susan

> The connection is that you should solve your problems with your wife.

Gordon

> I'll solve them, to the extent that these problems can be solved. By the way, I'm not sure I'll get to look into her eyes again. She was against my coming here and said that she may not be there when I get back.

Susan

> Where won't she be?

Gordon

> At home. She won't be at home.

Susan

> She threatened to leave you?

Gordon

> Yes.

Susan

> She threatened you because she wants you at home.

Gordon

> She was also afraid that something would happen to me.

Susan

> Did you tell her where you were going and why? To see the leopard man?
>
> *(A local man passes in front of them on the way to the bus station.)*

Gordon

> Yes. I should mention that in the past I've embarked on all sorts of crazy adventures. I've traveled to all sorts of

places for extended periods of time. I don't have the patience to sit at home for too long. Once I took part in a violent demonstration in Jordan, but that was something I inadvertently got involved in. This time I am doing it on my own initiative, intentionally.

Susan

What other strange experiences have you had, besides this demonstration?

Gordon

Nothing special. But this has done nothing to improve my relationship with my wife. She's tired of me pulling a disappearing act on her. I admit that I've been running away. I understand that now. But it was for the good of both of us. That's what I believed then. Now, suddenly, her threats…

Susan

Because this time you're putting yourself at risk.

Gordon

True. Therefore this time I'm afraid she may no longer be there when I return.

Susan

I don't think she'll leave home so quickly. I'm certain she'll be happy to see you. She was angry when you left because she cares about you.

Gordon

I also think she cares, but things aren't as simple as you make them out to be.

Susan

I don't think the problems are simple, but I'm sure she'll be happy to see you.

Gordon

> Happy until the next time. Meanwhile my wife isn't here and I'm returning to Abilda with you. Would you care to have dinner with me? Someone recommended a good restaurant not far from my hotel.

Susan

> If I don't find my friends. Because if I do, I'll probably be busy with them. If I don't, I think I'll go to the hotel to rest. I'll also have to find a doctor. So…

Gordon

> I'm talking about this evening, after you're done with the embassy and the doctor.

Susan

> I've limped enough today. I want to rest.

Gordon

> Don't you feel like enjoying a good meal after such a long time? I'll help you walk.

Susan

> Mr. Gordon, dinners like this lead to other things. You're married, I'm married…

Gordon

> But you're injured and hobbling. I'm certain it won't lead to anything!

Susan

> Maybe you're right. But I really do want to rest. Shouldn't you call your wife when you reach Abilda? Maybe she's still home.

Gordon

> I'll call her, but that shouldn't stop us from going out to get something to eat.

Susan

> If I don't find my friends, I'll probably be busy looking for them. Or calling home. Or arranging my trip home. So, I don't know…

Gordon

> You need help. You can hardly walk. Your ankle is broken.

Susan

> It's a sprain, not a fracture. But I actually do need help. And I do thank you for all your trouble.

Gordon

> It actually makes me feel good, this feeling of being able to help someone.

Susan

> It makes everyone feel good. You're not unique. Think about the fact that your wife also needs help. She's alone and doesn't know what's happened to you.

Gordon

> What about your husband? Does he know what's happened to you?

Susan

> No, he doesn't. But I plan to call him the moment I reach the capital. I also have a bit of explaining to do. I have no idea what I'm going to say. I don't have any good explanations. At least you said something to your wife before you left.

Gordon

> You can always blame your friend, what's her name? Betty?

Susan

> Do you think that's how I'll get out of it? It's not that simple. Come on, help me get up. Let's go to the bus station.
> *(Gordon helps her get up and they turn to head toward the bus station.)*

Aren't there any murderers in England whose eyes you can look into?

Gordon

Oh, there are. Not like the ones in America…but there are some…
(They exit.)

(Curtain.)